Covert Entanglements

A LAKE HARMONY NOVEL

TANJA WALTRIP

ACKNOWLEDGEMENTS

Covert Entanglements, the third book of my Lake Harmony series was a fun one to write. It also taught me as an author that if my heart isn't in a creative space, I need to take time to do whatever needs to be done before I can sit back down and bring the story to life. The only pressure is the one I put on myself. Thank you to my friends and family that agreed with putting the story on hold to find that balance. Hillary and Garrett's story reflects some of that personal journey through their snarky, yet steamy story, where I was able to find my joy again.

DEDICATION

This book is dedicated to my cousins and all the memories we've made while boating on Lake Norfork. We've jumped from the cliffs, been left in the middle of the lake with only floaties while the uncles go restock the coolers, and best of all shared our own laughs with our version of tubing Olympics. I love you and cherish those memories.

xoxo Tanja

PS- Enjoy the flashback!

This book is licensed for your personal enjoyment only. This book may not be resold or given away to other people. If you would like to share this book with another person, please purchase an additional copy for each person. If you're reading this book and did not purchase it, or it was not purchased for your use only, please return it and purchase your own copy. Thank you for respecting the hard work of this author.

No part of this book may be reproduced in any form or by any electronic or mechanical means, including information storage and retrieval systems, without written permission from the author, except for the use of brief quotations in a book review. To obtain permission to excerpt portions of the text, please contact the author at TanjaWaltrip.com

All characters in this book are fictional and figments of the author's imagination.

Published by Tanja Waltrip
Cover Design by: Getcovers
Website: TanjaWaltrip.com

CONTENTS

Chapter One

Hillary

It's already been a long-ass week, and it is only Tuesday. I had an event from hell over the weekend. My staff didn't show, food ran out because the host invited more people than she initially stated, and I am utterly exhausted from making the event spectacular despite everything. There are good and bad reasons for owning my own catering business, but the good outweighs the bad. I worked hard and put my time into learning the business as a lackey and answering to others—that's just not my style. I don't like to answer to anyone, so being my own boss is the best situation for me and, probably, everyone else. That's why I created A Matter of Taste, my brilliant and delicious catering business. We work mainly in Lake Harmony, the little community where I grew up, about 50 miles west of Chicago, but I do take on some catering for corporate events in the city. Luckily, I can be selective.

I can't take all the credit because I have an amazing assistant. He helps me organize the business and runs events if we double-book. Griffin is amazing and the best friend of Stella Stone, the little sister of my best friend, Julia. Griff makes everyone around him bend to his will, and, even though he is gay and proud of it, people respect him and his quirky behavior. He loves to flirt with all our friends. Thankfully, the men just go along with it and sometimes flirt back to make him blush.

"Hills baby, I'm heading out if you don't have anything else for me to handle today. I need to get over to Coops to set up for trivia night with Stella," Griffin says.

"Thanks, Griff. Did you finish checking stock on what we *actually* went through for Maureen's birthday Saturday? I know her numbers were way higher than our contract, and I want to make sure I invoice her accurately and get our supplies restocked."

"Yessir! She was about forty people over what your contract stated. I made sure to note that on her file, so you add the increased amount. Silly be-otch. She's lucky you always over-plan for things and had enough," he laughs.

"Griff, when have I ever not been in complete control of things?"

"Never, Hill. You are the queen and that, darling, is why I work for you. Ta ta until later. I expect you have been summoned by Jules to trivia tonight?"

"Yep, see you there in a bit. Just finishing up and then I'm going home and relaxing first."

Griff heads out with a wave and a quick "tootles." I rub my temples and let out a long breath. Good lord, I am exhausted. This can wait. I push my chair away from my desk, grab my coat, purse, and keys, and head out the door.

While driving home, I thank God for my business because my personal life is shit. I constantly try to put myself out there. If I don't, I'll never meet someone and probably be single forever. My best friends have wonderful significant others and are happily in love, and I still have to endure the losers I find through online dating. My God, why can't I just find a man who doesn't lie about his height or who is married and looking for an affair? I may be an adventurous woman, but I draw a hard line at dating a married man—no matter how sexy. I won't do that to another woman even if her husband is a cheating bag of shit.

***

Tonight's trivia is at Cooper's Corner, the Lake Harmony local bar and grill owned by Cooper James, retired Army Special Ops and Garrett Stone's best friend. "Coop" is super nice and one of the guys in our friend group. He started Trivia Tuesdays at Cooper's Corner a few months ago, and it's become a good excuse for us to all meet for dinner and drinks. I enjoy seeing my friends, except Julia's brother, Sheriff Garrett Stone. He's nearly always hanging out at the bar, deep in conversation with Cooper, and, as Sheriff, this is about the only place the townies know to leave him be when out of uniform. I know this because if we're both here at the same time, which is more often than not, he has this incredibly annoying habit of watching me and judging everything I do or say. Dick head. I'm tired of his eagle eyes always on me. He lost the right to worry about me months ago. As I walk in, I see Julia waving me over.

"Hey Jules, Jackson. Nice to see you guys," I say to them. They are the cutest couple, married sweethearts from high school. She's the town's go-to mother hen, and he is the town doctor. It looks like I'm one of the last to arrive. Ellen and her husband Scott, Sam, Paul, Rob, and, over at the bar, Garrett are all here. I nod to the other cute couple already here, "Bree, Dr. Noah. Did you guys have a great time in LA for the movie premiere with Jax? I can't wait to hear all about it."

Bree is so happy she nearly sparkles, her big eyes full of happiness, and she is literally bouncing in her seat. She and Noah talk about all the A-list stars they saw and how much fun they had. They share how "normal" the celebrities and rock stars all seemed to be and how it didn't feel weird after a while.

I say, "Well, some of us are normal. Not all of us," as I stare at Garrett, and he gives me a dirty look back. After that comment, I see Julia and Bree roll their eyes. *What the fuck was that?*

Talk about Bree and Noah's trip and all the fun they had continued. Jax Turner, who is originally from Lake Harmony and happens to be Hollywood's current leading man, invited them to his most recent movie premiere. He was in drama club as a student with Bree and wanted to show his appreciation for her encouragement and guidance. They had a blast and rubbed shoulders with some of Hollywood's elite.

Griff is getting trivia started and asks how we want to split up tonight—couples or guys vs. girls. Jackson votes for couples, because he and Julia are in a very handsy mood, and Rob bails out. He heads to the bar to hang with Cooper, which leaves me with Garrett.

"Fuck, I can't team up with the mighty Sheriff. He isn't going to compromise on answers, and we all know he isn't always right even though he thinks he is," I say and cross my arms.

"Fine with me. I don't want to deal with your temper tantrums anymore, Hillary. You and your bitchy attitude need to go. I'm sick of it. Everyone is sick of it," Garrett says.

Julia exhales loudly and she stands up abruptly, pointing back and forth at the both of us. "Listen up, you two. We have been listening to you bitch and moan at each other for months now." She looks at me, then Garrett, and continues, "We don't know what the fuck happened between you, and honestly, I don't think any of us give a flying rat's ass anymore, BUT…you are both getting on our nerves and, until you both can be in the same space TOGETHER like we all used to be, just go. Don't come back until making peace. I think I can speak for everyone sitting here, your best friends, by the way, when I say that we are exhausted by your behavior toward each other, and we don't want to be around it anymore. So, go. Both of you. Just. Go." She sits back down looking defeated, and Jackson puts his arm around her and pulls her close.

I stare at my friends, speechless. How dare they all gang up against me. What the fuck have I done to them. Don't they see I am more a victim here than Garrett? He's the one causing shit! "SERIOUSLY! Do you all fucking feel like this? That Garrett and I are getting on your nerves. Fine. Fuck it. I'm out too," I say before storming off and heading home.

***

As I drive home, I get even more pissed. What the fuck! This is all Garretts' fault. He's the one that Jules should've directed her hissy fit at. He needs to own this fucking mess and not me.

I try not to slam the door when I walk into the house, but, man, I want to! Instead, I take a deep breath, "It's fine, Hill. This too shall pass. Asshole." I head to the bathroom to wash my face and, throw on some yoga pants and a sweatshirt. The night isn't over yet, but, at this point, I don't want to see or talk to anyone. I turn my phone on silent, put it face down, and grab a wine glass from the cabinet. I will enjoy a glass of my favorite wine, watch HGTV, and try to calm down so I can sleep tonight.

Fifteen minutes and several sips later, there's a knock on the door. "Go away. Hillary is not home." *Knock knock.* If I ignore them, they will go away.

Chapter Two

Garrett

Well, that was great. I'm sitting at Coop's bar trying to enjoy a night with friends and Jules decides this is the right time and place to address the big fucking elephant in the room and put this fucking nightmare between Hillary and me front and center. Jules just told both of us that we are banned from hanging out with everyone until we can find a truce and work out our differences. That's like trying to snuggle a rabid cat with extra sharp claws.

Jackson looks over at me, "Listen, man, I don't want to know what happened between you, but we all know something did. You two need to work through it. She's hurting, and you are too. Go, talk to Hillary, and figure your shit out. You'll be better off. Make peace with Hillary and end this personal war against each other."

I run my hand over my face knowing I need to be man enough to try to figure this shit out. I stand up and apologize to everyone for ruining their night. Hopefully, Hillary didn't trash my truck on the way out.

I drive to her house even though I know she wants to kick me in the balls. First, for getting her kicked out of trivia with our friends tonight, and, second because she's still pissed at me about Memorial Day weekend. Fuck! This is going to be bad. I park my truck on the street in front of Hillary's house when I get there. I know she's home. The lights are on, and I can see the flicker of her television. Here goes nothing. I say a silent prayer that she doesn't have a weapon. *Knock knock.*

Through the door, I hear, "Go away. Hillary is not home."

My head drops back to look at the sky, I take a deep breath, and whisper to myself, "I guess I need to treat this like walking into the enemy territory." *Knock knock.* "Hill, please open the door. You know I can let myself in if you don't."

"Whomever the idiot is on the other side of that door can go fuck himself and leave."

"Hillary, you know it's me, and I'm not leaving until we talk face-to-face and not through this damn door. I'm going to count to five, and if I don't hear you unlock this door, I will open it myself." I start counting out loud. Of course, she waits until I say four to unlock the door. I smile to myself because only Hillary would push my buttons even now.

Hillary cracks the door and glares at me, "I am not letting you in, and if you even think of breaking my door down, I will call in your entire squad and let them know that the SHERIFF is here trying to attack me. How do you think that will look for you—huh? I'll also tell Gertie that you broke in and tried to get your way. So, I suggest you back the fuck off and leave."

I wait for her to finish her rant and simply say, "NO."

If looks could kill.

She draws in a deep breath, puts her hands on her hips, her eyes get squinty, and she is pissed! "NO? Seriously? NO? Fuck you, Garrett. Leave me alone."

Hillary tries to slam the door, but I put my foot in the way and again say, "NO."

Now, we are in a stare-down. There is no expression on my face. My time in special ops taught me to not show my emotions a long time ago, but Hillary's emotions are clear as day, and she would love to kill me right now. I wait, watching as her hatred fizzles into defeat. "Let me in Hill. We need to talk."

Without a word, she goes inside, sits on the couch, drinks her wine, and stares at the tv.

Instead of giving her space, I sit on the coffee table directly in front of her. "Hill, I hate that we're in this weird situation lately, but we need to figure out how to fix it, so we can be with our friends without fighting and making them uncomfortable." She doesn't respond, but I've known her since childhood, and I can see the wheels turning.

She looks directly at me with a snarky smirk and says, "FINE."

I know Hillary, and, at this point, I don't know whether to be relieved or to run out the door. "Fine? What exactly does that mean? We haven't talked about anything yet."

Hillary pushes me out of the way and heads to the kitchen to refill her wine glass. Leaning against the counter, she smiles, "We're going to make a truce Garrett. We are going to agree to play nice around our friends."

"Great. Let's talk about why you're so mad."

"I don't know that I will ever not be angry with you, and I don't want to talk about it, so we make a truce and lie that we worked it out. Deal?" she asks.

"You want to stay pissed at me and make a truce to fake that we worked everything? So, lie to our friends that everything is back to normal between us." I'm making a deal with the devil. I know this. But if I can get Hillary's normal personality while we're around friends, then maybe that will work in my favor, and, eventually, she'll stop being so damn pissed at me. "Fine," I say. Deal."

"One more thing," she says and grabs her phone. Hillary stands next to me, "Selfie time. Smile for the camera dickhead."

I'm in shock at this point, but I'll play along—for now—so, I smile while she leans into me and takes our picture. "Hill, what's with the selfie?"

"Proof of Truce. What did you think?" She shakes my hand, and says, "Great, now get the fuck out of my house, asshole."

Exhausted with everything, I leave, and before I even sit in my truck, my phone vibrates and there's a group text from Hillary to everyone.

Hillary: *picture* Selfie w Garrett

Hillary: You can all get off our backs now. We talked everything out and made peace. SEE. No hard feelings. Xoxo Hill (and Garrett)

Jules: Is this true or are you just using an old picture?

Bree: What she said-I don't trust you Hill
Jackson: For what it's worth I really hope you did talk things out, guys

Damn, let's see if they fall for it. I'm about to put my truck into drive when I get another text from Jackson, not on the group text chain.

Jackson: Glad you were able to smooth things out, now maybe you will put your big girl panties on and tell her how you really feel about her. Times a ticking. Do you want to continue to watch her date a bunch of random losers? Man up G. Ask her out.
Me: Let's just get through one step at a time J
Jackson: It didn't take you too long to work through whatever happened so maybe she feels the same way? Something already happened between you two. Maybe now you can move into new territory with her?
Me: I value my life too much right now to make another move
Jackson: I trust your judgment and am aware of Hillary's claws

Fuck. I need a drink. I better respond to the group chain to confirm our "Proof of Truce." I feel like this could be a total disaster.

Me: Yes, Hillary and I talked and we are FINE. Sorry, we caused all of you grief. It's done, we talked, and I look forward to spending time with all of you especially Hillary in the future.
Jules: Good. About time you guys worked out your shit. It wasn't any fun being around you both with that tension.
Rob: Awww-G&H are gonna play nice again *heart emoji*
Hillary: Told you so-now back off

Time to wait and see how this is going to play out. Knowing she is still just as pissed at me as before but thinks she can play nice with me under a fake truce will be fun. Just wait and see what I have up my sleeve, Hill. You think you played your cards to win tonight, but I'm the poker player in this game, not you. Game on, little lady. Since we have a truce, I am going to make you crazy wishing that you would have just talked to me. Now, I have no reason not to treat you like the best girl I know. Maybe killing someone with kindness, as my mother taught me, will be what gets Hillary to give up and talk it out like I wanted.

Chapter Three

Hillary

It's Halloween, and I don't have a lot of time this morning before the event I'm catering tonight, but I always try to make time for the girls. A quick breakfast of coffee and scones at Harmonious Bites, Ellen's café and bistro, won't take too much time. Plus, I need to sell the truce with Garrett since I haven't seen any of them since Tuesday's trivia debacle.

When I walk into the café, Jules and Ellen are already sitting in the back waving at me like idiots. "Hey," I say, "Do I need to put my order in or is my usual already waiting for me?"

Ellen laughs, "I knew you would be on time and in a hurry since you have an event later. Griffin already stopped by for his hazelnut latte and said you were on your way. I have your coffee right here."

"Thank you, sweetheart. So, where's Bree?" Before I can sit, Bree walks in looking a bit frazzled.

"So sorry for being late, guys," Bree says as she slowly sinks into a chair.

"What the hell is wrong with you? Are you sick?" I ask.

"No, I don't think so. I think I ate something bad last night. Not sure, but my stomach is off today. Ellen, instead of coffee do you have any peppermint tea? Or something that will help settle my stomach?"

"I do have peppermint. I'll ask one of the girls to brew you up a large cup with some honey. Be right back."

"Bree, maybe you shouldn't have come out but stayed in bed. You look a bit green," Julia says.

"Seriously, you guys, I don't have a fever, and, other than my tummy turning, I feel okay. I promise. I wouldn't come and expose you to anything. None of my kindergartners have been sick with the flu, so I think it is just something from dinner. Noah left early for a run, so I didn't have time to check with him to see how he was feeling but as he is out running, I guess it's just me."

Jules puts her arm around Bree's shoulders, "Go home after this and just relax today. Maybe you're doing too much. Snuggle up with the cat and Noah and watch some tv. If you don't feel better, let us know and we'll make sure you have some brothy soup or something."

Ellen comes back, and at the same time, Sam walks in with flowers in her hands. Sam is our other childhood bestie, and she and her husband own a greenhouse and landscape design company.

"Morning ladies," she says and hands out small bouquets of mums.

"Wow, what did I do to deserve this beautiful bunch of flowers Sam?" I ask.

"Hill, I just wanted to make sure my best girls know how much I love them. We just got a huge shipment of these fall mums and some had broken branches. I had to clean up the mums before selling them and trimmed off the snapped branches. I figured why not share them with you."

"These are gorgeous, Sam. Thank you so much. I'll put them in a vase in the kitchen so I can enjoy them. Josie and I are making sweet and salty popcorn balls to sell at the fall festival next weekend," Julia says. "Okay, now that we are all here, I want to talk to you, Hill. What happened with you and Garrett after you left trivia night? Did you honestly settle whatever's going on between you?"

"Don't you mean when you stood up in front of everyone and kicked us to the curb, Jules?" I say instead of answering the question.

"Well, come on…something snapped, and I just couldn't continue to watch my brother and best friend behave like jerks to each other anymore. We've all been friends since we were kids, and this has been going on since summer started. I only said what everyone else was thinking. I'm sorry if I hurt your feelings, Hill, but are you now friends again? You talked things out?"

"Yep, Garrett came over after you rudely kicked us out and we talked. It's all good. I sent you proof of the truce, and he confirmed via text the same night. So, you guys don't have to ban us from being in groups. We are fine. Just like before," I lie through my teeth.

"Good, I think I can speak for everyone that we're glad the two of you handled things."

"Things are handled. So, what else is new? I only have a few minutes before I need to go. I'm catering a huge Halloween bash tonight at the Golf Club, and I need to get back to the shop and help Griffin and my staff prep the food and pack up the dishes. We have to set up two hours before the event starts at six o'clock tonight."

***

I love my team, and I'm thankful everyone scheduled to work showed up. Tonight, because it's Halloween, we are wearing solid black instead of our usual whites. Griffin is, of course, walking around with devil horns on his head. The event is heavy appetizers and a dessert bar. The host wanted it to be finger foods so the guests can mingle and nibble on the food at the same time. Griffin is handling the mashed potato bar, where we're serving mashed potatoes in large martini glasses with a variety of toppings. The host wanted to make sure there was a vegetarian option and could also maybe help with the open bar situation.

Everyone arrives in costume and great moods. This holiday seems to be the one where people tend to migrate away from their normal behavior, especially if they wear a mask. And I would rather be here watching adults make fools of themselves than answering the door to trick-or-treaters. As much as I love kids, I never saw myself having a gaggle of my own. I watched Julia raise Josie and Daniel, and I was the fun aunt who let them do crazy things, take them to eat sweets, or give them wacky gifts their parents would later hate me for.

Bree is always surrounded by kids since she teaches kindergarten and runs the drama club. Between the two of them, I have had enough littles in my life. That baby-making clock can continue to tick and keep moving forward with no worries.

I walk through the venue keeping an eye on the food amounts. I stop and talk to the bartender. I like to hire Pete for large events because he knows how to work a room and leave with a lot of tips. He can flirt with men and women alike. "Hey Pete, how's it going? Do you need anything stocked?"

"Nah, I made sure to have two of the vodka, rum, and whiskey bottles under the bar. Those are the typical go-to choices. If I run low, I'll grab one of the staff to let you know, Hill."

"Great! I hope you're getting good tips. Keep me posted if you need anything."

Later, Griffin and I are standing in the far corner of the room discussing the worst and best costumes of the night. The host offered a prize to the best and asked us to make that determination.

"Hills, come on! Batman over there has some great legs. I wonder if he is a runner. Or wait, maybe a swimmer. His muscles are delicious. The lady who dressed up as Marilyn Monroe is looking fantastic with her titties. Do you think those are real?"

"Griff, I doubt it. They are huge and way too perky to be real. I have to agree, Batman is looking pretty sexy."

A man walks over in his Tarzan costume, and it's pretty clear he has enjoyed the open bar. "Hey pretty lady, are you dressed up to be a sexy witch or goth girl wearing all black?"

"Are you enjoying the party?" I politely ask.

"I'm enjoying it even more now that I found you," he says as he moves in closer and puts his hand on my ass.

"Sir, I'm going to ask you nicely to please remove your hand and go back to the party."

"Come on, sweetheart, let's take this party somewhere we can be alone. You've been standing over here just watching me for the last half hour. You know you want me, so let's go."

He staggers a little. I don't know who this asshole is, but I can't make a scene at an event I was hired for and piss off my client. Why did Griffin have to walk away to allow this guy to come to harass me?

"Sir, I am not interested in going anywhere with you. You need to walk away now. I am also going to let the bartender know you cannot be served any more alcohol tonight."

He stands up tall and takes his hand off my ass. "Who the fuck do you think you are telling me what I am going to do," he slurs at me.

"It doesn't matter if you don't like what this beautiful woman is telling you, sir, but I am the town sheriff here in Lake Harmony. I see you're making quite the scene over here. Did you happen to drive to this party tonight, sir? If you did, I highly suggest you don't try to drive yourself home."

"Fuck you, man. Nice *costume*, sheriff," he sneers at Garrett and walks away.

I raise my eyebrow at Garrett. "Please don't make a scene for me or the host of this party. 'Tarzan' is over-served, and if you want to wait until he gets into the driver's seat of his car and arrest him, fine, but go away. Why are you here anyway?"

"I came to make sure your event was okay, and I wanted to check on you. Plus, since we have a truce, it would be weird if I didn't check on you. I always check in when you have big events here at the club. I like to make sure you don't need anything."

"Truce, yes, but no one is here to see if we are being nice to each other or not. So again, go away."

"Ah, but you're wrong, sweetheart. If you turn to look towards what looks like a potato bar, Griffin is watching us and our every move. Better make it look good Hills because

25

you know that if we look like we're fighting, he's going to tell the gang, and your fake truce is history."

He gives me his biggest smile, reaches over, and pulls me into a hug. "Oh Hillary," he whispers into my ear, "you need to learn to play nice with me around the gang. This is good practice for the truce you wanted. Now smile back and look like you're happy I stopped by."

I tap his shoulder, and, with a smile, I lean in, "Get lost, Sheriff. I do not need your help."

With one last bear hug, he plants a big kiss on my cheek, "Later, Hill," and waves at Griffin before he walks out of the room.

Chapter Four

Garrett

It's been a week since I stopped that drunk guy from harassing Hillary at her Halloween event. I shouldn't be turned on by her stubbornness, but I am. I always have been. Her confidence has always been a trigger for me and draws me in. I'm not saying that she doesn't ever show a softer side. She does. She is just very particular about who is allowed to see that side of her. I used to, but since Memorial Day, I only get the prickly side of her now.

Today is the town's fall festival, and I'm on duty. It's a big event that provides a lot of money to our community. Gertie, our town gossip, and owner of the town Facebook page, Harmony Hears, posted a reminder today to make sure everyone is aware of festival happenings and what each area's donations will support.

LAKE HARMONY'S FALL FESTIVAL OF GIVING

Join us today at the annual fall festival supporting our own! Help a high school senior go to college, provide shelter and food for an animal, and support our own police force and firefighters, so they can continue to go into our schools and educate our children on safety. Listed below are ways you can donate and show your support-
Festival Parking: Town Scholarship for Graduating Senior
Vendors 10% Sales: Animal Shelter
Pancake Breakfast: Police/Fire Fund

I need to head over to the pancake breakfast at the community center. I'm on duty so I didn't take a shift cooking pancakes and bacon, but I do need to make sure I show up and be seen. Part of my job as sheriff is to do the "meet-and-greet" with the folks who come out for the festival.

As I walk out of my office, I say to Katy, my dispatcher at the reception desk, "Hey, I'm going to head out now and do my walk around town. Are you all set here for the morning? Do you have anyone coming in to give you time to go out and enjoy the festival today?"

"Hey, Sheriff. Yep, Jilly is going to come in and relieve me later. She was good with a few extra hours this weekend. I think she just wants to get away from a full day with her grandkids at the festival. She looked a bit relieved to take over this afternoon when I asked her."

"I think those young grandkids of hers wear her out," I chuckle in reply. "Glad you get to switch out for a bit. You can reach me on the radio if you need me. I better head out before the bacon is gone."

"Have fun, Sheriff!" Katy waves to me as I walk out.

***

The parking lot is full at the pancake breakfast. The Lake Harmony community always comes out in big numbers to support our own, so seeing this type of turnout is no surprise. A combo of our own fire and police people work the breakfast and mingle with folks while they eat. Of course, not everyone is here. We do need to keep some of our guys on shift to cover emergencies, but those with today off have given up their personal time to cover the breakfast without being asked. Usually, it's a great time to get to know people in Lake Harmony.

When I walk in, I immediately look over to the tables where they are dishing out the food, and there she is. Hillary is standing next to JP and flirting and laughing with Logan. I'm not worried about JP, who is my brother's best friend and married to a great woman, but we all know Logan is a smooth talker with the ladies. I watch as the two of them serve up plates and laugh with each other. Logan isn't holding back from touching Hillary—a hand on her shoulder, palming the middle of her back, leaning in just so—and she is just as handsy with him. What the fuck!

I sense more than see someone next to me when I hear, "Why don't you just tell her how you feel, G, instead of standing here being frustrated and jealous?"

I look over at my sister and try to keep calm. "Jules, there's nothing to tell."

"Come on little brother. You've always had a thing for Hill growing up, especially once we all hit high school."

"Jules, she didn't see me then, and she sure as hell doesn't see me now. Just drop it okay? It's not worth upsetting the group if I did go there and then things went to shit again," I remind her.

"You haven't put yourself in her sights to be seen, G. Except to tell her you don't like whom she dates. Have you once told her how you feel or let her know that you see her as more than just a friend, or my best friend?" Jules asks.

"Please, just leave it alone, Jules." I kiss my sister on the cheek and nod at some of the people who are waving me over. "I better go mingle—duty calls."

"Love you. Go mingle, Sheriff."

Chapter Five

Hillary

I love this time of year when Mother Nature turns the leaves into beautiful shades of reds, oranges, yellows, and browns. It feels like a last burst of energy—the grand finale. It's the time of year in the Midwest when we pull out our jeans and sweaters and warm thick coats. It's still warm enough to be outside and enjoy the fresh air, but a cozy, warm cup of hot chocolate or fancy coffee makes it even more worthwhile.

Lake Harmony's fall festival brings all that, plus the community comes together to make donations to areas that can always use a little extra. It's my favorite time to check in with the vendors and see if there are any interesting early Christmas gifts I can stock up on. My favorite vendor has caramel apples and kettle corn. I always buy something from him to enjoy later.

The girls and I planned to meet up after the pancake breakfast to walk around the town square together. I'm already sitting by the fountain when the rest of them walk up. I smile and wave as they get closer.

"Hey ladies, don't you all look cute today bundled up? Since I beat you here, I decided to enjoy hot cocoa while I waited. Bree, did you ever get over that stomach stuff? I hope you are feeling better now." I say.

"Yeah, better than ever. Thanks," she answers with a big smile.

"So, do you want to walk around the square and check out the vendors then maybe grab a late lunch?" I ask them.

"Sounds good to me, and since neither of us has events tonight I want to have a glass of wine with my lunch," Julia says.

"OH Yes! Me too," Sam answers.

"Hey, Hill, how did you end up getting stuck helping out at the pancake breakfast?" Jules asks.

"Oh, when I got there, they couldn't keep up with the line, and Logan and JP asked if I would be willing to help the cook whip up a bunch of pancakes. Plus, it was a lot faster to make the bacon in the oven, but the guys didn't know that trick. Once, I got a few dozen pancakes made, I was having such a great time with them, and I stayed to help keep the line moving along. You guys know I love Logan. He is the sweetest funniest guy around, and, man, he gives the best bear hugs I have ever had. You know me, if there is a need for a cook in the kitchen, I can't walk away. It would be sinful to ignore someone who needs my skills. Bonus for me to be surrounded by good-looking firemen too."

Bree puts her arm through mine, and we keep walking. "Oh my gosh, I love Logan. He is the best Mr. Safety we have ever had. When he comes in to do the fire safety assembly at the school, he always makes time to come into my kindergarten class and meet my kiddos. He wants them to feel comfortable and not be afraid of him or a man in uniform in case they are ever in danger. He is so funny and charming."

"That he is, Bree, but don't forget about that big rock weighing your left hand down," I tease her.

She laughs, "No worries, Hill. I love Noah and nothing is ever going to keep me from marrying that sexy doctor. I promise I will mow down anything in my path to get to him at that altar."

"Good girl. We can't allow the good ones to get away."

Julia pipes up, "Hill, I saw you at breakfast having fun with the guys. I was standing with Garrett, who was also watching you, and, if I didn't know better, he was acting jealous."

"Right. Garrett was jealous! You're crazy. Just be glad we can finally breathe the same air again, Jules," I respond with a snort. "Nope. I am on a man break. Between the horrible online dates and strange, drunk men groping me at my catering events, I am on an official man hiatus. D-O-N-E. Done. I'm going to take a little time to be selfish and only worry about myself. I don't have the energy to put anything into a relationship right now. Maybe after the holidays, but, for now, I am happy with my single status. It's tough enough being the last one standing when all of you are happily in love."

Bree tugs me in closer, "Aww, Hilly—we love you, and we don't want you to be alone. We have enough love to still shower you with it. You know that saying: when you're not looking for something, that's when it usually finds you. Go ahead with your plan. It isn't selfish, though. It's putting yourself first, and, sometimes, that's exactly what we need to do for a fresh restart. I support you two hundred percent!"

"I love you Bree, but it's probably good you aren't a math teacher."

"Stop being bitchy, Hill, and just humor me. OOH, look at that cute vendor with chocolate. Let's go!"

We all laugh as Bree drags us over to the chocolate vendor, and we watch her buy almost fifty dollars' worth of goodies. We nearly drag her away because every time she says she is done she adds something else to her purchase.

The next vendor has cute little Christmas ornaments, and we each buy a couple. Every year, we try to add the same ornaments to our trees in solidarity with our friendship. This year, we decide to go with the skiing Santa ornament.

"Hey, this reminds me," Julia says. "Jackson and I were talking about doing a trip up to the ski cabin before Christmas. Just adults to get away before the holidays. Now that Hill and Garrett are back on speaking terms, it doesn't put that weirdness in the air. What do you guys think? Can you all get away the weekend of December tenth?"

Remember Hill, I silently mutter to myself, we have made a "truce" with dickhead, so you better make this believable. "Um, yeah. I need to double-check my calendar to see if I have any events. If it's just one a day, I can ask Griffin to handle anything scheduled—depending on what it is. When do you need to know?"

"Oh, whenever. We are for sure going, and I think Bree and Noah are in. Jackson got some weird emergency coverage so both he and Noah can be away from the practice at the same time. I still need to ask Ellen and Scott, Rob, and Cooper. Sam, what about you and Paul? What do you think?"

"Let me check with Paul, but I think it would work," Sam replies. "We have a newly retired veteran who's been shadowing me at work so we can have someone handle the shop when I take time off or need to work on different projects away from the greenhouse."

Julia smiles big, "It would be fun if we could all get away again together. We missed out last winter because there was no snow. Hopefully, this year we get lucky with the snow. If not we can just do some hiking or something."

We continue to check out the rest of the vendors. No more talk about going away together in a month—thank God! We start feeling chilled and decide to head over to the golf club for lunch since downtown is overrun with the festival crowd.

***

After ordering lunch, Bree straightens up in her seat and smiles at everyone, "Do any of you have dinner plans tomorrow? Noah and I want to put some steaks on the grill and have you guys over for a quick dinner. We haven't been able to really celebrate our engagement with all of you or entertain much at our house."

"I'm open, what can I bring?" I ask.

"Oh Hill, would you mind bringing your cheesy spinach dip? The one that's all warm and gooey and you eat it with chips? That sounds so divine," Bree says.

"Sure, you must be hungry right now," I say with a chuckle and watch Bree blush.

She answers, "I'm so hungry, I'm about to eat my arm off."

34

"Okay, Bree. Just give them a few minutes to whip up that double cheeseburger and fries you just ordered. You sure have an appetite today," I say.

"I know! It's a bit ridiculous."

I love these women around this table. We have been friends since elementary school. I would do anything for any of them. Do I feel bad lying to them about this truce with Garrett? A little bit. But only because I can't stand the thought of not being with my friends. What they don't know won't hurt them. Garrett and I can manage to be civil towards each other when in the same company. At least, I can. Who knows what dickhead is capable of. I'm still pissed at how he acted when he showed up at my Halloween event. If he thinks he's in charge and can tell me what to do, he has another thing coming.

I head home after lunch. I'll see them again tomorrow with their significant others, so I decided now's a good time to be "selfish," enjoy a glass of wine, and binge some HGTV. I deserve it.

Chapter Six

Hillary

Once I get home, I quickly whip up a double batch of the cheesy spinach appetizer that Bree requested. I also add some artichoke hearts, and, instead of chips, I include a toasted baguette. Too many men will be there to serve it with skimpy chips. I know he is going to be there, and he better be on his best behavior. I didn't sleep well last night, and I don't have the patience to play nice and make it look like we have honestly patched things up. I plan to stay on the opposite side of the room. Then I won't want to strangle that man with every look or word that comes from him.

I need to jump in the car soon, so I'm not late, but I hear my phone go off. I better make sure it isn't Bree wanting me to bring something else. I grab my phone and see a text.

Garrett: Are you going to dinner?

What does he think? That I'm too cowardly to show up at my friend's house for a BBQ just because he'll be there?

Me: Yes

Maybe I'll get lucky, and he'll be the one to bow out of going.

Garrett: Better put your nice mask back on then

Damn him. Why does he always have to poke the bear?

Me: I am always nice to the people I care about. Does that make you jealous?
Garrett: Nope

Me: You no longer fall in that category so just stay away from me, dickhead.
Garrett: Aw, Hill, are you struggling with our truce
Me: Never- I can easily fake anything with you!

There. That should shut him up and make him think. Ugh, time to go before I am late. Why does he always have to have the last word?

***

So far so good. Staying on opposite sides of the room or in a different room from Garrett seems to be working and I don't have to put a fake smile on my face. Stupid truce! I'm in the kitchen helping Bree and about to take the last thing to the table when someone slowly moves in behind me. I know who it is, and I don't need him playing games. I feel him lean in over my shoulder, "Mmm, that smells delicious. Do you need any help bringing more out to the table? I told Bree I would come in and check so she could sit down. She was looking a little worn out."

"Sure," I slide the dish to the left of me. "Takes this out and go sit down."

"Okay, Hill, just for you," he says into my ear.

What the hell is he up to now? Why is he playing games with me when there is no one in the room to see this shit. Damn it, Garrett. Stop being such an ass. He grabs the dish and heads out of the room. I take a deep breath before I head to the table myself. I need a drink.

***

After a delicious dinner, we are spread out around the table finishing the brownies Bree made for dessert when she moves over to Noah and sits in his lap.

"Noah and I are so happy that all of you were able to come by today for dinner on such short notice. Since we have you all here, we thought we would share our news. We decided to get married on Thanksgiving weekend, and we hope that you will all be around to join us in our celebration. We're going to keep it small—close friends and family only. Anyway, we consider everyone around this table our family, and we can't do this without you."

Everyone starts congratulating them at once and talking about how happy they are for Bree and Noah. They went through a lot during the beginning of their relationship with Bree's character and career being jeopardized for writing a romance novel. Now they have a wedding to look forward to.

Noah puts his hand up to get our attention. He looks at Bree and kisses her temple, "We have another bit of news." Both are bursting with excitement the joy on their faces. "We are also expecting a baby!"

After that news, everyone rushes over to give them both hugs and congratulations. Once everyone calms down, they tell us that they weren't trying to get pregnant, but figured if they wanted to try to have a family they should start soon and stop worrying about birth control. Neither of them was prepared for it happening immediately, but they were both very excited and that was why they wanted to have a small wedding soon so they could focus on their new family and Bree's pregnancy.

***

After the food and dishes were sorted and put away, the girls went into the family room to talk, and the men went outside to smoke the cigars that Noah had for after the announcement.

Bree was glowing. Now, last week's sick stomach and crazy appetite were making a lot of sense. "Bree, I'm so happy for you and Noah. I cannot wait to have a little baby to spoil and love again. It's been a while since Julia had Josie or Daniel. Jules provided those two beautiful babies for me to love, and now I get to be Auntie Hill for another beautiful baby."

Bree wiped at the tears falling down her cheeks, "Aw, Hill, you are the best Auntie ever. I'm a little nervous, but I know I have all of you to help me be the best mommy possible."

Julia smiles, "Bree, I would love to have your wedding at Harte of Harmony. When I get home, I'll pull up the calendar and see what's scheduled. I know we have a wedding planned for that Saturday in the event building, but I think that's it. Do you know what day you're thinking about?"

"Since we want a small intimate wedding, we were hoping that we could do it on Thanksgiving," Bree replies. "I know that sounds weird, but everyone there will be family, and most of us will be together already anyway. Noah and I thought we could have the ceremony early, then for our meal do Thanksgiving dinner. We don't want anyone to have to worry about the food. And, Hill, we aren't asking you to cook. We'll get someone else to cater, so we can all enjoy the day."

"I don't have anyone coming overnight until that Friday, so Thursday, Thanksgiving Day, is wide open and all yours," Julia says.

My best friend is getting married, and she doesn't want me to worry about cooking. Um no, that's not happening. "Jules, once we know how many will be attending this awesome wedding, I would like to be able to use your event kitchen to prep and cook dinner. I know Bree doesn't want me to worry about the food, but I will be more worried if I don't have control over it. I can hire the best of my staff to help me so that it won't be a big deal. The turkey and most sides for Thanksgiving can be prepared the day before, so all we have to do is shove everything in the oven the day of." I look over at Bree, "Please let me do this for you. I won't take no."

Crying like a big baby now Bree smiles through her tears, "Thanks, Hilly. I would love that."

"Good, now that that's decided, you have about a week to figure out how many we'll be feeding, then we can talk about what sides you want to go with the turkey." I feel good about this, and it will distract me and help me get through another wedding with very happy people.

"There is something else I want to talk to you about," Bree says and looks around at all of us. "Would you guys please be part of my wedding? I know it'll be small, and my bridal party would consist of all my guests, but I really want you standing up there next to me. It wouldn't be the same if you weren't. We aren't going to have time to do the traditional bridesmaid dresses so you can wear whatever you want, but I just really need my best friends surrounding me that day."

We all get up and give Bree a much-needed group hug. She is crying hard at this point. "I don't even know whom I have to give me away. It's not like I have a dad to walk me down the aisle," she says.

Julia puts her hands on Bree's face and wipes her tears away, "Oh honey, you don't need a dad for that, and if that's what you want, you always have mine. You know he considers you one of his own. But I have a better idea. Why don't you ask your mom to walk you down the aisle? You two have always leaned on each other, and I think that would make her happy."

"I love that idea, Jules," Bree says and with that, her sadness disappears and she is excited all over again. She wipes her tears and blows her nose, and then she smiles. "I don't know why I didn't think of that. I'm obviously not doing things in a traditional way, considering I got pregnant before my wedding, but I love that idea. I will ask Mom to walk me to Noah at the wedding. I will have all my best friends and their significant others walk in and stand around me in a circle and my guests can join them too! I love this. It's going to be amazing! Thank you, girls. I am so lucky to have all of you in my life. Okay, since we have about two and a half weeks, do you mind if we move this into the dining room and start hashing out some details of what all needs to get organized? Holy Cannoli! I'm getting married and having a baby!"

Chapter Seven

Garrett

After the wedding and baby announcement, Noah gave all the guys cigars, and now, we're on the deck relaxing around the fire pit, smoking and sharing in his excitement.

Noah sits back and exhales smoke from his cigar. "A year ago, I was so unhappy living in Chicago and working for a medical practice that felt so robotic. Jackson, I want to thank you for calling me and offering me a partnership with your practice. Moving to Lake Harmony and meeting Bree has changed my life in ways I never imagined. I'm marrying the most amazing woman, and we're going to have a baby! I never thought I would have all this. I know I have only known the rest of you for a short time, but it feels like a lifetime. I hate to sound like a sap, but I love you guys. I expect you all to be there when I say, 'I do' with Bree. I can't imagine that day without all of you."

"I'm so glad you accepted my offer, Noah. Julia said to me, even before you moved here, that she hoped something would spark between the two of you. Looking around at all of you sitting here, I feel the same way. You are all brothers to me and mean the world to me," Jackson says.

Rob laughs, "Oh shit—if any of you start crying, I'm going to take your man card away!"

"Hey bro, let them have their moment. This was a big day full of announcements. You should be so lucky to have what they have," I say.

Jackson jumps in, "G, now that you and Hillary fixed whatever the hell happened between the two of you, are you finally going to man up and ask her out?"

They are all waiting for an answer. "What are you talking about?"

"Come on, G. We all know you have a thing for her. Why else do you annoy her and always end up at my bar when she's on another one of her online dates?" Cooper asks.

So, even my best friend is going to throw me under the bus. "Coop, you know I just want to make sure she's safe."

"Keep telling yourself that, G. I watch the way your eyes don't leave her when she's around. Although, tonight it didn't seem like the two of you were ever in the same space. What's that about?"

"What? A lot of us are here, and we've all spread out around the house most of the night. The girls were helping in the kitchen, and we were all around the grill. Why? Are you suggesting we're avoiding each other?"

"Nothing, man. No worries," Cooper says and looks at me like he knows there's more to the story.

Rob leans forward, "Garrett, we all see it," he gestures to the guys and they all nod in agreement. "We know you have a thing for her. I guess what we are wondering is when you are going to finally make a move. What are you waiting for?"

"She doesn't see me like that," I tell them. "I'm just the friend who's always in her way or telling her what I think. Do you want me to go there, try to make some kind of dumb move, and then we're back to the two of us barely able to be in the same room together?"

Noah says, "Garrett, I'm not sure whether you should or shouldn't, but if you don't take the risk, you'll never know. Trust me. It's easy to think life is great as it is, but taking that risk… Yeah, man, I can't imagine my life if I didn't take a risk and fight for Bree. Don't let more time slip by."

Jackson adds, "What if the next online date isn't such a loser or the next event she caters she meets someone that could be the one? Can you live with the regret of never taking that risk?"

***

I'm home, settled in my recliner, trying to enjoy the whiskey I just poured myself, and thinking about our guy talk earlier. Do I want to take that chance? How the hell do I do that when we haven't cleared the air? We need to talk things through, then, maybe I can take that risk. If I do anything now, she'll only think I'm using the stupid truce to push her buttons. Fuck, I have no idea how to handle this anymore. I grab my phone.

Me: Were you staying away from me on purpose?
Hillary: Yep
Me: Come on Hill. Let's talk about it
Hillary: Nope
Me: Here any time you want to talk
Hillary: Nope

Fuck! She's so damn stubborn. I wish Memorial Day never happened. We wouldn't be in this awkward situation where the girl I have always loved doesn't even want to be near me. How the hell did I let things get this bad? My doorbell rings. Who the hell is here on a Sunday night?

I open the door to my best friend. "Hey Coop, what's up?" He pushes in past me, and I laugh, "Sure, come on in buddy."

"Pour me whatever whiskey I know you have in that glass, G. We need to talk," he says.

I follow him and grab him a glass of whiskey on the way to the family room. "What do you want to talk about? Did you miss me already? I just saw you at Noah's."

"Cut the shit, G. First of all, you know I read a situation just as well as you. Even better," Cooper says, hinting at our previous life as active-duty special ops. "You may be able to snow your friends and brother, but you can't fool me. What's going on between you and Hillary? I know you said you talked it out and things are fine, and you can keep lying to my face, or you can tell me the truth."

I run my hand down my face. "Coop it's all bullshit," I say. "I went to talk to her after my sister blew up at us at your place during trivia night. She barely let me in the door, and once I got in, she told me to fuck off and said we were going to lie to everyone and say we talked things through. But honestly man, she wants to put my balls through her meat grinder."

"That sounds more like Hillary. But why did you cave?"

"You know she's it for me. I don't know how that will ever happen, but at this point, I would rather take her faking to be my friend and be around her than not have her in my life. I figured I could warm her up during this fake truce and get her to start acting like I wasn't the plague if I went along."

"Aw, man. I think this is going to blow up in your face," Cooper says. "We both know she's a stubborn woman, and I don't think you're going to get her to bend."

"Probably not. But right now, I'll take her any way I can get her. I'm still working out the details. I was trying to kill her with kindness."

Coop starts laughing. "I don't know if there is enough kindness to get through Hillary's defenses but if you find a way you let me know."

"Fuck you, Coop. I know this is crazy, but I don't know what else to do right now. Just…keep this to yourself, please. If word gets out that she made this fake truce, she will come after my balls and I'd kinda like to keep them." I cover my crotch for emphasis.

"I've got your back. So, what's next?"

"Trivia night couples!" I say to him with a smirk.

"Okay, but I don't want any blood spilled in my bar."

"Shut up and drink your whiskey, and then I'm kicking you out."

Chapter Eight

Garrett's High School Graduation

I'm in my cap and gown with my parents and my brother, Rob, and sisters, Julia, Ellen, and Stella. We take what feels like a million pictures, and my smile is starting to hurt my face. I'm the first son to graduate high school. But that's not what's making everyone so emotional today. I decided that before I joined my dad and became a partner at Stone's Builders, I needed to do more. I needed to make a bigger difference. So, without my parents knowing, I enlisted in the army. I have a couple more days before I ship out to basic training. After that, who knows where I will end up.

My parents were shocked and concerned that I wanted to join the army. I needed to do something more than just follow in my dad's footsteps. I had a couple of good football scholarships to colleges, but I didn't want to play football. I was eighteen, a man, and I needed to make my own path because college wasn't the route I wanted to take. I would do my mandatory time, and, if that was enough, I would come back to Lake Harmony and be part of the family business.

We had a big graduation party following commencement. We were expecting a lot of friends and family to show up, and I was prepared to say goodbye to most of them. The army was going to take me away from them for a while.

My sister's three best friends were there with her. Julia was having the hardest time with my decision. She's the oldest of us kids, and, even though I was bigger and stronger than her, she always felt like she had to protect me. Her best friends Bree, Sam, and Hillary were like sisters to me, and they too always kept their eyes on me. I returned the favor and protected them the best way I knew how when needed.

Out of all of them, I had a special place in my heart for Hillary. If things were different, I would have told her by now how I felt about her. She was a year older than me, and she was my sister's best friend. There was an unspoken rule to not dating your sisters' friends. So I didn't. But one day I would tell her how I felt. Just not yet. What could she see in me now? I'm only Julia's little brother who was part of the gang.

The party lasted into the evening, and it trickled down to just our regular gang sitting around the bonfire. The adults all left or went inside to give us some time to hang out together privately. I was dreading saying goodbye to the ones left here tonight. These were the closest people in my life—my family and friends whom I loved and would do anything for.

Julia and the girls already had one year of college under their belts, so leaving everyone and everything wasn't a new concept to them. They had already done it last fall, but this, heading into the army. That was different. I couldn't just come home to see everyone when I wanted to. There was no spring break. My life, my time, wasn't going to be mine to schedule for a while.

As the minutes ticked by, I started to feel the heaviness weighing on everyone. This was scary. I was going into the army and could be sent to fight in a war one day. We didn't know what was in store.

Jackson was the first one to speak up. He was my friend and also my sister's boyfriend since high school. "I am proud of you, G. I don't think that I would be brave enough to do what you're doing. I promise that while you are not here, I will keep the girls safe and be there for them in your place. I will miss you like crazy."

I couldn't say anything. My throat and my voice were tied up in knots, and I didn't want to let them see me lose control. I nodded my thanks to him, and he understood.

"You better include Rob in that too, Jackson. We all know with G gone, little Rob is going to get in trouble with the ladies and not have anyone to bail him out," Hillary adds.

Leave it to Hill to break the mood and get us all laughing again. "True. You know with me not here to protect him, he is gonna get his ass kicked by some dude for messing around with the wrong girl," I laugh with my friends.

"Hey now, the girls love me. Come on, with my blue eyes, dark hair, and charming personality they can't stay away from me. How was I supposed to know Sheila Farnsworth was dating Chuck Bilby?" Rob says.

I sigh, "Just stay out of trouble Rob." I look him in the eye. "I can't be here to fix things, and Jackson goes back to school in the fall. You're going to be the man of the house now, with Dad, and I won't be here to cover your ass. Plus, you need to keep an eye on our sisters. They need you to man up now, okay."

"Okay, G. I got it. I've got you so don't worry."

Bree smiles and comes over to sit on my lap, "Garrett, when are we going to see you again?"

"I go into the recruiter's office this week, and they'll shuttle me to base a couple of hours away. I go through processing and take my oath to serve. Mom and Dad are coming to that, but it's only a few hours. From there, I get sent to the base for my basic training. The first few days there I go through medical exams and get my uniform and haircut and other details I'm not too sure about," I tell her.

Bree takes her hands and plays with my hair, a pout on her face, "Oh no, your beautiful dark locks are going to get shaved off!"

"Just hair, it will grow back. I'll be at basic for about ten weeks."

"That's a long time, Garrett. Are you scared?" Bree asks.

"No. I'm prepared, and I've worked with the recruiter a lot, so I think I know what to expect." I look around at all my friends and family. "I didn't make this choice lightly you guys. I know it may sound scary, but I'm ready for this, and it will be okay."

"You're right. You'll be just fine, and we will all be sitting here again with you when you get back. This is just for a little while." Bree gives me a big hug and then goes back to her seat.

"Garrett, when will you come back?" Jackson asks.

"I don't know. It depends on where basic training takes me. I don't know how I test or what direction I'll be headed until I get there and start going through it. I may have a quick break to come home after basic, but I can't promise that. It's a game of wait and see."

I can't be honest and tell my family and friends that I hope to become a ranger and do special ops. They would be in complete panic mode if they knew I was hoping that my testing, skill, and strength would qualify me to be in the elite group of rangers.

"Basic training isn't dangerous, so don't worry. That's where I will learn how to be a soldier and get to know army stuff like discipline, fitness, teamwork, combat skills, and weapons. They are going to wear me down and see what I'm made of. The only sucky thing is you can't call or text me. I'll be unavailable most of the time. We have to go back to the old days when we write letters and notes to each other. At least, you can email. I just won't always be able to get it right away."

"Garrett, I promise I will write to you every week, no matter what," Julia says. "My letters may not always get to you on time, but just know that they are coming. I'll fill you in on what's up at home and everything else so you don't have to feel alone. I promise I will do whatever you need me to do for you in the next couple of years. I don't want you to ever worry about what's going on here. I have it covered." She looks around at all of us sitting there. "We all will fill in for you. Just be safe and find what you need to find. We will be here when you get home."

I can't take much more of this, so I stretch my arms above my head and act like I am tired. "I appreciate it, guys. Thanks for coming to spend time with me before I head out. I couldn't ask for better people in my life. I'm going to head in, okay? I have a lot to get together before I head to basic."

Everyone gets up and they all quickly hug and say goodbye and head out. I'm left standing there alone since I told them I would make sure the bonfire goes out. A few minutes later I hear someone coming back down towards me and I turn. I see Hillary. She smiles. She is so beautiful. "Hey, I thought you left."

"I did, but I turned around and came back," she says.

"Did you forget something Hill?"

"Walk me back to my car, G," she says.

"Sure, come on." I grab her hand and walk her back to the front where her car is at the end of the driveway. When we get to her car, I stop and turn her to face me, "Hill, what's up?"

She puts her hands on my face and looks up at me, "Garrett, promise me you'll be safe."

"Hill, it's only basic training. I'll be fine."

"After, when you find the most dangerous situation you can, promise me you will always be careful and that you will come back to me in one piece."

I'm looking into her sad eyes and watching the tears roll down her cheeks. "Aw, Hilly. I'll be okay. Don't cry, sweetheart. I promise. I'll come back." I wipe away her tears and gently brush my lips against hers. I feel her suck in a breath, but she melts into me and kisses me back.

She pulls back and wipes her eyes, then moves to open her car door. Before she sits down, she stops and looks over her shoulder, "Remember, G, you promised." Then she drives away.

What the heck just happened? I'm about to leave for who knows how long, and I finally kiss the girl of my dreams. Fuck!

Chapter Nine

Hillary

It's Tuesday and as expected I'm heading over to Cooper's Corner for our trivia night and casual dinner with friends. When I walk in, Garrett is at the bar talking to Coop. "Hey, am I the first to arrive tonight?"

"Hey, Hillary. Just you and G so far," Cooper says.

"Who's coming out tonight? I know Bree and Noah are out because she's exhausted. I think Jules and Sam are planning on heading over, though," I say.

Cooper says, "Let me get a table ready for all of you. Be right back."

Garrett looks at me. "Hey, Hill. You look nice tonight."

I stare at him and try to figure out what he's up to. "Thanks. Flattery will get you nowhere."

"Aw, come on. Play nice tonight. I already told Griffin we're playing couples, and you're my partner," Garret says.

"Why would you do that? I didn't say I'd be your partner. What if Rob comes? I could be his partner," I shoot back.

"He's not coming. He's got a date tonight. Better get your smile on because Julia and Jackson just walked in. You don't want to let them see you looking annoyed with me, do you? They may question our truce and we can't have that can we?" Garrett asks.

I smile and say through my teeth, "You're such a dick, Garrett."

He smiles, stands up, and puts his arm around me, then whispers in my ear, "Nah, just showing everyone that we are buddies again."

Julia and Jackson walk up to us, and Julia says, "Hey guys, it's so nice to see this. The two of you goofing off like always. Do we have a table ready for us, or should we get a drink at the bar first?"

"Coop's getting a table ready," I tell them. "Looks like just the four of us are here so far, so you probably have time to grab a drink now while we wait for the rest of whoever is coming. Bree said she's staying home; she's tired from work today."

"Aw, I remember being pregnant with my kids and being tired pretty early," Julia says. "Remember, Jackson? It seems like I was passed out on the couch by eight o'clock most nights."

"You were always exhausted when you were pregnant, but you refused to leave me downstairs by myself. I would just cover you up with a blanket and you'd snore through most of our shows every night."

Julia pushes Jackson, "I don't snore."

"Okay honey," he answers and gives her a quick kiss.

"Alrighty, love birds, Coop has our table. Let's go sit, and you can order your drinks there."

When we get to our table, Garrett says, "I told Griffin we're partnering up as couples. I've missed being partners with Hill. Plus, we both like to win, so it'll be fun kicking your asses!"

"Fun," I say, with a hopefully not-forced-looking smile.

We sit down, and Julia grabs her phone and frowns, "Oh, looks like it's just the four of us. Sam just sent me a text that she and Paul are staying home. They just closed the shop and aren't coming out. So, looks like a couple's trivia is on between the four of us. This should be fun. Ready?"

"You bet! Should we make a fun little wager? Losers buy winners' dinner," Garrett says.

Jackson replies, "Game on!"

***

Halfway through trivia and a pitcher of beer, things start to get interesting. Our scores are close, but Julia and Jackson could pass us if we don't keep getting the answers. "Come on man, you need to focus. We need to win this thing and make the Hartes buy our dinner. Don't be an idiot and blurt out the answer again so they can steal it," I say to Garrett. "I did no such thing. I whispered it into your ear, and YOU were the one that then said it out loud for them to hear. Don't blame me, Hill."

"It wasn't me. Keep your mouth shut unless you have the answer!"

"Whatever, Hill. Fine. I'll take the blame like always," Garrett grumbles.

Julia and Jackson are whispering to each other and staring at us. "What? What's going on over there?" I ask.

"That's what we would like to know," Julia says. "The two of you have been kinda' hostile with each other tonight, and we're wondering if you're forgetting you made up and falling back into being nasty to each other. I thought you two talked things through. Whatever's going on tonight, I don't like it."

Garrett pulls me close, "Nah, Jules, we're both just super competitive and like to win. You know how Hill gets about winning. She's just frustrated. We know she can be a sore loser."

My body goes rigid I'm so pissed. "Garrett, be careful about whom you call a loser. But he's right. No harm here, just being competitive and stubborn. You know how stubborn Garrett can be. He doesn't take direction well." I look over and wink at him, "Right?" You think you can push me right now in front of Julia and Jackson, you have another thing coming, buddy. I glance at Julia and Jackson. "We're playing a game. When have we ever done this calmly?"

Julia relaxes. "Okay, I just…I don't want to see things go back to the two of you at each other's throats again. I love you both but that was horrible. I'm sorry, I don't mean to keep bringing it up."

"No worries, but you do know that you and Jackson are going to be buying our dinners."

Chapter Ten

Hillary

We're in Chicago shopping for a wedding dress with Bree. She found a trunk show that's also selling sample dresses. Since she only has two weeks until the wedding, she's determined to find and buy a dress to take home with her today. Thank God she's a size eight and should be able to find something that needs a few alterations.

"Do you know what kind of dress you're looking for, Bree?" I ask.

Bree is bouncing she is so excited. "I want something sexy but also simple. Since this is a small wedding and more intimate, I want something timeless. I don't need a huge skirt or tons of beads or lace. Something elegant and soft that makes me feel beautiful. I can't do anything too tight because I feel bloated these days with the baby and these boobs."

I put my arm around Bree, "You could never look anything but absolutely beautiful and I only see you glowing with happiness."

"Aw, Hilly. Please don't make me cry. Thank you for saying that. I love you so much."

We walk through some of the vendors and ask to see samples they have in Bree's size, hoping we can find something she can buy and walk out the door with. The first few booths only seemed to have big, flashy Cinderella dresses. That wasn't at all what Bree was looking for, so we kept going.

After the second row of vendor booths, Bree starts looking a bit defeated. "I haven't seen anything that fits what I am looking for, and we only have a few vendors left."

Julia grabs her hand, "You know what? I need something to drink. There's a little concession area over there. Why don't we take a quick break and then finish up with the last row of vendors?"

Bree nods, "Yeah. Maybe I just need to take a moment to sit and catch my breath. Let's get a drink. Do you think they have any cookies?"

Laughing I say, "Go check. I'm going to run to the restroom, and I'll meet you over there. Can someone order me a drink too?" Julia gives me a thumbs up, and I wink and walk away. She probably knows exactly what I'm going to do and will keep Bree occupied with Sam for a few minutes.

I head to the last row of vendors, quickly marching through, checking to see the types of dresses hanging on their racks. What the hell is with all these ball gown-type dresses? How the hell do you even get through the doorway wearing one of those? By now, I've got an idea of how the vendors show their dresses. They usually have one of each style hanging on a rack. The goal right now is to find something that is simple and flowy yet still classic. Towards the end of the row, I find a vendor that has a few dresses exactly like what I think Bree is looking for.

"Hello, can I help you find a dress?" the vendor asks.

"I hope so. I'm shopping with a bride-to-be today, and she's having a difficult time finding a dress with a simpler silhouette. I see you have a couple of dresses that might meet her criteria. What do you have in the samples that are a size eight, or even a ten, if it only needs simple alterations?"

The vendor gestures for me to walk to the rack with her. "I have three dresses that fit that description. Let's check on what sizes I have in that style." She holds up a dress, "This one is chic but romantic, made of chiffon with a sleek square neckline and with dramatic voluminous long sleeves that cuff for comfort and versatility. As you can see the structured bodice goes into a full flowing A-line skirt." She hangs that dress back on the rack and grabs a second. "This dress has long sleeves and a deep V-neck in an embroidered floral pattern, which makes it romantic yet modern with the sheer illusion bodice that meets a sleek fit-and-flare skirt to highlight curves." She turns it around, "My favorite part of this design is the sultry scoop neckline in the back with covered buttons, creating a classic look." Moving to a third dress, she says, "This design is a newer look in ivory lace with a natural waist, deep V-neck in front and back, and sheer lace long sleeves in an A-line silhouette. Do you think she would like any of these?"

I am almost giddy with relief for Bree. "YES! They are all beautiful. Please, whatever you do, do not sell any of these in her size in the next ten minutes. Let me go grab the girls, and we'll be right over. You do not know how happy I am that I saw you over here."

"Please don't rush. My name is Sylvia, and I'll put these in the dressing room for you. Let's make this a little bit more fun for your friend. Bring her over and we'll do a little fashion show."

"That would be amazing," I say. "I'm Hillary and the bride is Bree. Thank you, Sylvia. I think Bree will find what she's looking for here."

I quickly walk back to find the girls. Jules looks up I approach them, and I wink and smile. She knows. She knows I found something. "Sorry, whew! Long line for the restroom."

"No worries. We were just telling Bree not to worry. We still have vendors to look at," Sam says.

"Yeah, when I was coming back from the restroom, I saw a vendor we haven't been to yet. It seems like she has non-Cinderella-style dresses. We should go check her out first. Maybe she has something that will catch your eye, Bree," I say.

"Oh really? I hope so. I need to leave with a dress today, and so far, they all have these big hoop skirts. I can't wear something big and fluffy like that. Can you imagine," Bree says laughing. "I swear my boobs get bigger every day. I can't have big boobs and a big bottom at my wedding."

"Come on, goofy. Let's find you a dress for your big boobs and get you home. I think you're close to hitting the wall." I grab her hand, and we walk to Sylvia's booth.

"Sylvia," I say, "this is our beautiful, bride-to-be best friend Bree. I think she's ready to see the dresses you have."

"Hello, Bree. It's a pleasure to meet you, and congratulations on your wedding! I spoke with Hillary earlier, and I pulled some dresses for you. Do you think you are up to trying a few on?"

"Absolutely. I will put myself in your hands, Sylvia. Show me the way." Bree goes to the small dressing room with Sylvia and takes the first dress into the changing room.

I look over at Julia and Sam, "I think she'll find a dress here. I ran through all the vendors and finally found this booth. Sylvia has three dresses with a simpler silhouette like Bree wants. We already pulled them. They are all in her size and ready to walk out with her if she finds one."

Sam hugs me, "Hillary, we would be lost without you. She was almost breaking down when we grabbed a drink. Thank goodness they sold cookies. We just kept shoving cookies her way until she seemed to calm down. I know she's stressed, but if we can find a dress today that will take the biggest to-do off her list."

Julia hugs me too, "You are a rockstar, Hill. I know between the rest of us, the wedding planning isn't an issue, but she wants to be a beautiful bride for Noah. I think if we can find her dress, she will be ready to hand over the reins and let us work out the other details so she can just focus on her classroom and getting to the wedding during the beginning of this pregnancy. Oh look, here she comes."

Bree is smiling when she walks out with Sylvia, "Hey guys, this is dress number one. What do you think?"

She's wearing the dress with the big, cuffed sleeves but a simple bodice and skirt. "It's beautiful, but the real question is what do you think?" I ask.

"It's pretty. Maybe a little too simple for me, though. I'm also afraid that my boobs look ginormous in this dress with the straight-cut bodice. And it doesn't give me too much room to GROW. Okay, keep this in mind because it is beautiful. Dress two coming up."

The three of us agree that the dress was beautiful but maybe not the one. Bree comes back out with Sylvia. Now, she's wearing the dress with the lace top, low scoop back, and fitted skirt. We all have big smiles on our faces. "Oh Bree, that one is pretty. You are gorgeous in that dress." Julia wipes a tear off her face, and Sam's lower lip is quivering.

Bree smiles, "So far, this is my favorite. It's so romantic but has a modern feel to it. I love the scoop back and all the little satin buttons that go down the back. Okay, one more."

She walks back to put the last dress on, and I look over at my friends, "Jesus you two. Are you both crying now?"

"She's so beautiful and that last dress…oh my God, Hill, that's the one. Let's see what else is coming but that dress is amazing on her," Julia says.

"I agree. It was so pretty," Sam adds.

While we wait for Bree to come out with the last dress, we talk about the wedding and all the details. She's getting married inside the Harte of Harmony in the event space in the house. We will only be about forty guests total, so we'll use one side of the event space as the ceremony site and the other side for tables. That way, while we eat, we can be setting up the other side for music and dancing. We're talking about the menu when Bree walks back out, this time with a veil on her head and still in the second dress.

Julia, Sam, and I all look at each other, and Bree starts laughing. "I couldn't do it. I've said yes to this dress. I didn't even try the third one on. Sylvia went to grab a few veils for me to try on, and I kind of liked this one. Anyway, what do you think?"

The three of us stand there looking at our beautiful friend in her wedding dress and all start to cry.

"Stop crying you guys. You're going to make me cry, and all I do lately is cry," Bree says.

The three of us fold Bree into a big group hug, then all four of us cry. I hear sniffling and even Sylvia has tears rolling down her cheeks. She mouths to me, "*She is so lovely.*" I smile and nod because there is no one more beautiful or sweeter than our Bree.

Julia wipes her eyes and says, "Okay. I think we have the dress. You are beautiful, and Noah will be picking his jaw up off the ground when he sees you. Let's get this dress off you and head home so you can put it away."

"No way," Bree says.

We all stare at her. "Bree, what the hell are you talking about now?" I ask.

"I can't take this dress home. Are you guys crazy? One of you has to take it home with you. I can't let Noah see it. It's horrible luck if the groom sees the dress before the wedding. Someone else take it home, please. Hide it and guard it with your life."

"Oh, Jesus, Bree! You just gave us all a heart attack!" I say.

We thank Sylvia numerous times and Bree gives her about three bear hugs before we leave. Thank goodness we found the wedding dress!

Once we're in the car and heading back to Lake Harmony, Bree sends Noah a text that she found the perfect dress, and, before we know it, she's sleeping with her head against the window and a smile on her face.

Julia looks at me in the rearview mirror and smiles. "Looks like the bride is already out. Thank goodness we found a dress. Way to go, Hill. I was getting worried that we weren't going to find something today, and I didn't know how much longer she was going to stay calm."

"She is stunning in that dress," Sam says.

"When I ran through that last row trying to just find someone that had more than those damn hoop dresses, I saw that vendor. Her dresses were all the same elegant silhouette, and I ran over there as fast as I could, and we quickly went through choices. I had a feeling that was the one that she would pick. If I was getting married, that would have been the one I would wear. Did you see the smile on her face when she came out with it for the first time? She looked so happy and gorgeous. Now, let's hope her boobs don't explode in the next two weeks, or we'll have to tape them down!"

Chapter Eleven

Garrett

I'm meeting the guys over at the new rental house Rob and I picked up. After I left the service, my brother, Rob, and I decided to start buying some homes around the lake to use as rentals. Most of the houses are on yearly leases, but we keep those close to the lake for short-term rentals for people who want to enjoy a cozy summer spot on the lake and all that the area has to offer. Since we're only about 50 miles west of downtown Chicago, many people stay in Lake Harmony to get away to the "country" to relax. Not quite. But, I suppose, compared to Chicago, Lake Harmony feels like the country.

Our newest rental is a cute three-bedroom cape cod with a great view of the lake off the back deck area. We want to build a fire pit for the chilly nights for our guests, and we asked the guys if they'd be willing to help since the girls are in Chicago looking for wedding dresses. Jackson and Noah are planning on coming. Coop's too busy running the bar today, but I'm sure I'll stop by there afterward for a beer and burger.

Rob and I are already here with all the materials in the back and marking the space where to put the pit. "How far back off the house do you want to go?" he asks.

"Not too far. I want it to be close enough that if we decide to add a hot tub it still looks like it's all one big outdoor space," I say

"You sure you want to add a hot tub? Those things can be nothing more than a big headache, Garrett. Plus, I don't want to be grossed out by what we may find in it," Rob says.

"Rob, not everyone thinks a hot tub is for sex. It's nice to have for a winter renter. They can sit out here and still enjoy the lake but be warm. I don't know. It's just an idea. Nothing we need to go buy now. We have the interior done. I just want to get the pit built today and put those Adirondack chairs around it. I think it would be great for families that come out for a break."

"Jackson and Noah just pulled up. You want to talk about anything before they walk back here?"

I glance at my brother, "About what?"

"Oh, I don't know…what's going on with you and Hillary? Hearing things may not be so smoothed over. Julia said you two are still a little prickly with each other."

"Nope. We're fine." Great. Julia is still questioning us. I guess it doesn't matter. It wasn't my idea to act like everything is fixed. Hillary can own this one when it blows up in our faces.

"Hey, we're here. Put us to work," Jackson says. "Noah is on call so he may have to run to the hospital, but I am all yours today."

"Thanks for helping, guys. This will move a lot faster with more manpower to set these pavers out. Rob and I already marked out where we want to put the fire pit, and all the materials are back here. We have to start digging out the pit about eight inches or so and level it off. Once we have that done, we'll add a sand layer about two inches thick. At least, we don't have to worry about a slope with this one like at Mom and Dad's place. We're going to use the retaining wall blocks around the edge and a little more gravel around the perimeter and on top of the sand in the pit. We also have six chairs we need to put together. Figured we'd divvy it up and get to work. So, how about two of us on the pit and two on the chairs?"

Jackson smacks my arm, "Works for me. I'll work on the chairs with Noah. Then, we can move the pavers into place and finish it up together."

"Rob, start digging while I show the guys where the chairs are and see what they need to put them together." While my brother starts digging and whining that he has to do the manual labor, I take the guys back up to the garage where we stored the new chairs. "I appreciate you guys coming to help. It will make this go a lot faster than if it were just Rob and me."

"Honestly, Garrett, knowing Bree is with the girls looking for a wedding dress makes me a nervous wreck," Noah says. "She was barely holding it together when they picked her up. She's so worried she won't find one with only two weeks to go. I told her I would marry her if she wore a burlap sack."

Jackson looks at Noah with a smirk, "Is that what you said to her? Aw, man…how'd that go for you buddy?"

Noah replies, "Not well. I had the best intentions with that comment, but she took it very negatively. I was backpedaling trying to get her to relax and smile again. Honestly, I don't care what she wears if, at the end of the day, she is my wife. Burlap sack, wedding dress, or shorts and t-shirt. It doesn't matter if she's happy and smiling. I'll do anything it takes to make her happy."

"I'm sure she'll find something. She has the girls with her, and they won't let her down. Hillary would steal a dress for Bree if that's what it takes," I add.

"Speaking of Hill," Jackson asks, "I'm supposed to ask you what's up between you and Hillary? I know Jules asked at trivia when things got heated, but come on man, it doesn't seem all that different than when the two of you were fighting. Have you made peace with Hillary?"

I rub my hand over my face and say to my friends, "It's complicated. It's not as bad as it was, but it's not awesome either. Just give me a little time to sort through things. You know Hillary takes time to deal with, and right now she is still fighting with herself over being friendly with me. I promise we're working on, it but it's not going to get fixed overnight. Please just keep Jules out of it, though. Her stirring the pot only causes more issues between Hill and me. No one wants to deal with that."

"I'll do what I can, but you know your sister. If she thinks something needs fixing, she has trouble staying out of it. I hate to see you going through this, though, especially because I know you've had a thing for Hill for a long time. I just want you to be happy like the rest of us. You deserve to have what we do," Jackson says.

"Thanks. But before I can even think of going there with Hill, there's a lot of baggage we need to work through. Just give us a little time to do that and keep my sister out of it. She'll only piss Hill off more and Hillary will shut down," I tell him. "Okay, let me show you the chairs, so I can get back to Rob and this fire pit. Although, I like that little brother is doing the hard labor with that shovel."

"Let's go build some chairs and get this done," Noah says.

Chapter Twelve

Hillary

We knew Bree would never agree to a bachelorette party. So, instead, we coordinated a spa day with the girls, her mom, and Ruby Stone. We've all enjoyed time at the spa for one reason or another, and we never say no to some girl time pampering. Today is no different than our previous spa days, except we have some of the moms with us this time. We're all scheduled for manicures, pedicures, facials, and massages. Right now, we're taking a break and enjoying a light lunch of finger sandwiches and fruit salad and discussing the following week's schedule including the rehearsal dinner, Wedding-Thanksgiving, and all the details to go with that. Bree is feeling better a little further into her pregnancy, and she isn't so dizzy and queasy anymore.

"Bree, I feel so lucky to be here with you girls and Ruby," her mom says. "I've always wanted the best for you, and Noah is such a lovely man. I'm so happy you found the man of your dreams and I'm also going to be a grandma soon. You're going to be the best mommy."

Bree hugs her mom, "Aw, thank you, Mom, you made me cry." She giggles and wipes her tears, "I wouldn't be the woman I am without all of you here with me today. You girls are like the sisters I never had. We've been through so much together over the years—since elementary school when we became best friends. Ruby, you've always been like my second mom welcoming me with open arms. I'm so very lucky to have you all in my life, and I can't wait to share this little baby with you. He or she is going to be surrounded by love and people that will always be there."

"Okay, enough of the crying. You know I hate to cry, so stop it." I laugh through the tears I quickly wipe away, "The wedding is this week, and you have your dress, your food, and your location. Now…I think we need to give you your gifts." I walk over to the table to pick up the gift from us girls. It's stunning lingerie for under her dress for the wedding and a little something for her wedding night or honeymoon. "Here, start with this one." I hand her the wedding day box.

Bree opens the gift and pulls out the white lace and silk bra, panties, garter, and stockings. "Oh, snickerdoodles, this is beautiful you guys." Blushing, she smiles, "Noah isn't going to know what hit him."

"That's the point, honey," her mom says. "Girls, that is gorgeous. Well done."

"That is very sexy. Having that on under your wedding dress should put a big pep in your step, sweetheart," Ruby says.

Her mom hands her a little gift. Bree opens the box and moves the tissue around. She lets out a little gasp and pulls out blue earrings. "Oh, Mom, these are lovely," she says wiping more tears away.

"Those are your grandmother's sapphire earrings and your something blue," Bree's mom explains. "She got them for a special birthday from your grandfather when I was a young girl. Before she passed, she asked that I give them to you for your wedding day so that a part of her would be with you. I didn't know Noah was going to buy you a Princess Diana ring for your engagement, so it feels kind of perfect now doesn't it?"

"It feels like Gram had her own way of putting Noah in my life. She always told me to follow my heart and that anything I wanted would be put in my path, but it was up to me to see what those things were, or I'd miss them. I am so glad I saw Noah in front of me, but, yummy, he is kinda hard to miss. I will wear these for the wedding and anytime something special is happening in my life so she is part of the moment." Bree is crying and blowing her nose again, "I miss her so much."

"I know sweetheart, me too," her mom says, giving Bree a big hug and tearing up herself.

Ruby puts a small box on the table in front of Bree, "This is your something old. I saw it in the antique store and thought it would be something you may like."

Bree opens the pretty gift from Ruby—a beautiful, beaded clutch and, inside it, a delicate lace-edged handkerchief with a stitched B in blue. "Oh Ruby, how stunning. I love it." Bree stands up and hugs Ruby then gives each of us a big hug. "Thank you all so much for these amazing gifts for my special day."

"Bree, you aren't done yet. There is one more gift for you from your besties." I hand her the last present, which she slowly opens. Inside is a gorgeous nightgown and robe set. It's made of silk and lace and the sleeves of the robe are trimmed with light feathers. It's a shimmery dusty pink and the nightgown has a V-neck cut and straps that lead to an open back all trimmed in delicate lace. Bree slowly rubs the silky fabric and pulls out the set, holds it up, and blushes.

"Hmm…getting any ideas for your next book?" I ask.

Bree writes romance novels when she isn't teaching. She just published her first novel, but, knowing her, she is already working on the next story.

"Oh ladies, this is absolutely to die for. Is this for my wedding night?" she asks us. "I may wear this every night once Noah gets a peek at it. It is so soft. I love it. Thank you so much! This is very extravagant."

"We thought this would be good for your research and your book ideas," I say.

Bree blushes some more and looks at the two moms, "Well… um, yep. Good for research or whatever."

"Don't be embarrassed, we may be older and wiser, but we aren't dead honey," Ruby says with a wink.

Oh yeah. I know Julia's parents still have a steamy relationship. Even during our weekend Stone Dinners, to which we're all invited, we see them holding hands, giving each other kisses and sexy glances. They are the perfect couple, even after forty-five years and five children together.

"Okay. Well, I'm a little embarrassed, but Ruby if I can live my life with the outcome that you have, I will be a very lucky woman. I don't intend to have five kiddos, but a long life with the man I love, and at least with this kiddo here growing big and strong in my tummy. Yeah… if I can have a touch of what you do… I will be a very lucky woman."

Chapter Thirteen

Garrett

Instead of a bachelorette party for Bree, the girls decided to enjoy a day at the spa, so Noah asked for a man-cave type of day with the guys—meaning good whiskey and cigars. Jackson, Rob, and I picked up the cigars and whiskey, and Cooper had the restaurant kitchen whip up lots of wings, sliders, and fries. Noah wanted it to be an old-fashioned boys' day, eating, drinking, and smoking things that are bad for us.

Jackson is hosting since Noah's brother, Hunter, lives in the city. Along with the usual gang, Hunter, Noah's dad, and my dad are here. Griffin also joined in making sure we all have a drink in hand. He's taken a particular interest in Hunter and has been flirting with the "new meat" in the room. Hunter is a good sport and keeps telling Griff he likes women, but he does have a hot friend he could hook Griffin up with. So, that took the conversation in a whole new direction. Now they're planning on how to get the two of them together.

The two dads are a bit off to the side with Noah, and they look like they're deep in discussion. I gesture with my head to Jackson, and we make our way over to make sure the pressure isn't too extreme.

I say to Noah, "You all look deep in thought. Is this a happy wife-happy life discussion?"

"Son," my dad says, "You know if you keep the woman in your life happy, things tend to run a lot quieter. You grew up in a house full of women, so if you haven't learned yet, I have failed you."

"Dad, if there's one thing, I think both Rob and I have learned from you, and growing up surrounded by sisters and all their girlfriends is that you don't poke a hornet's nest unless you want to get stung. Noah, are they giving you some good tips on fatherhood? That one I can't say I have experience with."

Noah smiles and looks completely at ease in his surroundings, "Honestly, I'm so lucky I get to marry Bree, but I never really thought I'd have a child. I'm getting older, and I wasn't looking to marry someone significantly younger. But, if I looked at my timeline, I was getting pretty close to not taking this step. I am going to spoil my kid so hard!"

His dad laughs, "Yeah, but not any more than your mother and I will. We were starting to give up hope of ever becoming grandparents with any of you kids. Your brother will probably never give up his bachelor ways, and your sister still hasn't found someone worthy of her. Not only do we love Bree, but next year we will have a new baby in the family to love. We couldn't be happier for the both of you."

Rob comes out of the kitchen and says, "Man don't make me get all emotional. This is supposed to be a bachelor party. If we aren't going to have strippers, then please have mercy on me and do not cry. I don't think I can take it guys."

"Jesus! Who's crying? Is someone crying over here?" Hunter comes busting over with Griffin. "Stop it right now! Drink a whiskey or six and smoke a cigar. Let's stuff our faces with the delicious food Coop brought. Griff and I just set up a poker table. So, anyone wanting to lighten their wallet should join me after you eat."

"You're right, bro. Let's get the drinks flowing, enjoy the food, and the cigars smokin'," Noah says as he heads over to the food. "Damn, Coop, did you make my favorite garlic parm wings? I may not share those with the rest of you."

"Yeah, man. But I made plenty, and I threw in some of the buffalo style too. I think there are enough for you to share with the rest of us, and, if we run out, I'll just make a phone call. Load up your plates and enjoy. There's more staying warm in the oven," Cooper says.

***

Everyone cleared out already, but Noah and I are sitting out back enjoying another cigar with Jackson.

"That was great, guys. Thank you for making it special. I wonder how the girls enjoyed their day?" Noah asks.

Jackson looks over, "I got a text from Jules earlier that they had a wonderful time. Bree was happy and emotional, but she enjoyed herself. The girls left the spa and are relaxing at your house until we head out of here. I'm supposed to let her know when you leave for home, but she said no hurry. They're enjoying girl talk without the moms."

"Cool. I am glad Bree got pampered a little bit. She never does anything for herself, and between the wedding and the baby, I worry she's going to wear herself out. I don't know how she stays on her feet with her kindergarten class all day. I would be exhausted, but she always comes home with a smile and tells me about her kids."

"You know she's going to slow down and get more tired as her pregnancy catches up with her, Noah. Just make sure she doesn't overdo it in that last trimester. Maybe she can increase the amount of parent help in the classroom, so if she needs an extra set of hands, she has them," Jackson adds.

"That's probably a good idea to start thinking about that. Diane, her principal, has already told her she can probably get a volunteer or aide in her room as her due date gets closer. Thankfully, she's going to be able to finish up most of the year with her kids, and she plans on going back in the fall. I told her to just see how she feels. It's not like she couldn't take a break from teaching and stay home if she wanted to. Focus on the baby and, when she has the time and energy, writing," Noah says.

"Yeah, now that she is in her writing zone, she may decide to go that route," Jackson replies.

We sit there, drink our whiskey, and smoke our cigars in silence. We don't feel the need to fill gaps with talk as we're each lost in our own thoughts.

"I'm going to head out. Jackson, why don't you give Jules the all-clear? I'll take off before Hill drops Bree off. I'm sure Hill doesn't want to see me tonight after having a nice day," I say.

Fuck! Damn, whiskey. I opened my mouth and said how I was feeling instead of remembering we have that damn friend truce. Maybe they didn't catch that.

"What the hell does that mean?" Jackson asks. Both he and Noah are staring at me.

I sink back down in my chair and rub my hand over my face. "Fuck, well…" Yeah, I'm screwed. They know something is up. "Do not tell your women." That's all I say before I say another word, and I wait until they both nod.

"Garrett, what is going on with you and Hill? Is this stupid fight still going on?" Jackson asks.

"Do not, and I mean do not, tell your women, but, yes, the fight is still going on. I tried to talk to her that night Jules bit our heads off at Coop's, and Hillary was not having it. In typical Hillary fashion, she decided she can control our situation by having a fake truce. When we're with our friends, we act like everything is fine. That way, she isn't excluded from social things with all of you."

Jackson looks at Noah and then back at me, "And how's that working out for you?"

"Fucking isn't. I cannot get through to her. The only time I see her is when we're together with all of you. Otherwise, she hates me," I reply.

"What the fuck happened between the two of you to make it so bad? Is it nothing that you can't discuss and fix? I hate this for you, man. I can see she's important to you," Noah says.

"Guys, I have tried. She absolutely refuses to discuss what went down, and I'm not going to go into those details with either of you. She basically tells me to fuck off and die. She wants no part of me in her life and only tolerates me with this fake friend truce. I'm trying to get through to her. I promise I am. But, right now, if anyone interferes, I'm afraid it'll blow up in our faces even more. You know how Hillary is when she feels threatened or wronged. She holds a mega grudge, and it takes her a bit to thaw.”

“We won’t say anything to the girls, but I’m going to be honest here, Jules already has her suspicions that something is still off. You know she won’t leave it alone if she thinks you both are hurting. Better figure out a way to fix this before it’s taken out of your hands by your sister,” Jackson says.

“Will do, just give me a little more time,” I tell him. “I don’t want anything to implode before the wedding this week. Keep you both posted but not a word to my nosy sister please.”

Damn whiskey, I should have kept my guard up better around my buddies. And, with that, I go home.

Chapter Fourteen

Hillary

The wedding rehearsal went beautifully, and the bride and groom look happy in love surrounded by their friends and family.

The food for tomorrow's Thanksgiving wedding reception is prepped and ready for my staff to throw into the oven. Tonight, we're enjoying a quiet post-rehearsal dinner at Harte of Harmony but aren't going to linger long since tomorrow is Bree and Noah's big day.

The couple stands up and clinks their spoons on a glass. "Excuse us, everyone. We would like to thank all of you here for being part of our special day tomorrow. Most of you in this room played a special part in bringing us together, and we love you for that. We are so blessed to have you in our lives." Then, they go around the room giving hugs and speaking to everyone directly.

Julia sits down next to me. "Hey."

"Hey, Jules, what's up?"

"They look so happy, don't they?"

"Yeah, they do and they deserve to be."

"That they do. I'm sure you have the food set and ready for tomorrow. What time are you having your staff here to get it all cooking?" she asks.

"A couple of my cooks will be here in the morning to get the turkeys going. The rest of my staff will come just before the ceremony. I thought we would offer the guests a pre-ceremony champagne. For those that want to indulge, anyway. Why not? Right? Tomorrow is a holiday," I say.

"That sounds wonderful. Do you need anything from me? I'm happy to help with anything that still needs attention. What else do you have up your sleeve?" Jules asks.

"Why are you asking me that? Should I be guilty of something Jules?" I say with a raised eyebrow.

"No, unless there's something you want to tell me?" Jules replies.

"Nope, all good," I tell her, then change the subject. "I've come up with drink specials, a cranberry martini, and a Manhattan, in their honor for the wedding festivities. That way, Bree can have a mocktail and not feel like she is missing out."

"Oh, that's cute. I love it."

Julia and I sit for a bit, looking at everyone around the room, and she says, "I love seeing Bree so happy. Noah is perfect for her. He helps push her out of her comfort zone a little bit. They balance each other. Don't you think?"

"Yes. She deserves to be happy, and I like them together. Especially after the year she had. I love to see her smiling so much, and I can't wait for that little baby to arrive. It's been a long time since we've had little ones to spoil."

"I know! This baby isn't going to need a thing with all of us spoiling it rotten. Is everything else okay, Hill? You don't seem your usual feisty self."

"I'm good, just trying to make it all perfect for her," I say.

"Okay, you know I'm here if you ever want me to listen." Again, she gives me a curious stare. What the hell is up with her tonight?

Garrett approaches our table. "Hello, ladies. Hillary, you look beautiful tonight. You too, sis."

"Thanks," I say with a bit of annoyance, "Please excuse me. I need to go check on something."

I walk away from that nightmare about to happen. I'm not in the mood to deal with him tonight. It's bad enough that we have to walk into the ceremony together, but like everything else, we always get paired together. I tried to walk in with Rob, but Noah made such a big deal about Rob walking in with Stella that I didn't want to upset him.

The ceremony tomorrow will be beautiful. Bree and Noah have everyone paired up and they asked all couples that will be at the wedding to walk in and stand around them. We set up a barrier with potted mums and greens in a circle that we will stand around with the bride and groom in the center. Noah will be waiting in the circle with the minister, while Bree is escorted in by her mother. Bree and Noah wanted to get married with everyone special surrounding the ceremony. It won't be more than twenty minutes long, and they each wrote their vows to share. The only person not standing still around them will be the photographer taking pictures of and videotaping the ceremony. The ceremony will be romantic and magical, and I know they will remember it forever.

***

I'm relaxing in bed after the rehearsal dinner when my phone goes off. I hope Bree isn't a nervous wreck.

Garrett: I don't know what I did to upset you tonight, but you made Julia question your actions. You better be ready to fake it more convincingly tomorrow if you don't want this fake truce blown. No worries, Hill, I covered for you. Told her you were probably feeling a bit lonely.

Ugh! Screw you, Garrett. He's right, though. All he did was tell me I looked nice, and I nearly bit his head off. I guess all the lovey-dovey mood in the room got to me tonight. Better get my game face on for tomorrow.

Chapter Fifteen

Garrett

It's Friday night after a busy week, and we're all heading into the city for a Mumford and Sons concert. We got the tickets before we knew we'd have an unexpected wedding yesterday. But, since Bree is a teacher, the newlyweds are putting their honeymoon off until winter break so she doesn't have to take extra time. We all love this band and try to see them live when possible.

The wedding was great, and my friends are happily married and expecting their first baby next year. Now, if I could just get my life in order, things would look good. That seems like a tall order these days.

We took two cars into the city and are now in our seats with beers in hand. Bree and Noah are wrapped up in each other's arms looking like the newlyweds they are.

"I love seeing these guys. They always make my heart sing," Bree says.

"I've never seen them babe, but I am looking forward to it," Noah says.

Yeah, you can almost see emoji hearts floating around their heads. I'm happy for them. Honestly, I am, but I wouldn't mind having Hillary wrapped in my arms looking at me like that and not like she wants to wrap me up in steak and throw me into a shark tank. Of course, she is in the seat as far away from mine as possible again. I wonder…maybe, I can get Jackson to switch with me. I lean forward to catch his eye and send him a text.

Me: Hey-switch spots with me
Jackson: What's up?
Me: I want to be closer to Hill
Jackson: Sure that's safe
Me: Taking my chances and gonna fuel her w beer

Jackson: Good luck

"Hey, I'm going to grab a few more beers. Does anyone else need a refill?" I ask.

"I'm good," Noah says.

Rob gives me a thumbs up that he wants a refill. "Gotcha. Be right back." I head out to grab two beers, and as I move past Jackson, I lean in, "Feel free to take my spot while I'm gone."

"You are a brave man," he says with a chuckle.

***

I also bring Hillary a new beer and take the empty seat next to her. We're singing along with the band and dancing in our seats. It's almost like she doesn't remember she hates me. She's too focused on having a good time. Rob goes to get more beer, and I tell him to get me two. One for me, and one more for Hill. I may as well keep this ball moving.

The night continues, we keep singing, dancing, and drinking while our reactions become a little less on point. I can tell Hillary is letting down her guard. I'm finally seeing glimpses of the girl I once knew and loved.

The concert ends and we head back to the cars talking about how much fun the show was. Thankfully, Bree is one of our designated drivers and Jackson is the other. We are about to separate into our two cars when I put my arms around Hillary and kiss her on the cheek. She pulls out of my arms so fast that it gets everyone's attention.

"What the fuck are you doing? Just because you filled me up with beer tonight and got me drunk doesn't mean that you can take advantage of me as you did before. You can just go ahead and fuck off, Garrett. FUCK OFF and SHIT YOURSELF."

Hillary stumbles backward and climbs into the car. Everyone, including me, is in shock. Only Jackson and Noah know about our fake truce, so the others are wondering what the hell they just witnessed. Noah gently pulls Bree toward their car, and Jackson takes Julia's hand, but Julia holds her ground.

"Excuse me, Jackson. Stop," Julia says to her husband. She turns to face me again, and stares for a moment, then quietly, so Hillary who is in the car can't hear says to me, "Garrett, we are going to discuss this later in private. No excuses. I'm done with this shit. Do you hear me? We've let you try to fix this, but now I'm taking over. Get in my car and leave her alone tonight. Just leave this alone for now. Trust me, please."

"Like I have a choice?" I ask.

"No, you don't. Not anymore. Come on, let's not ruin a nice night. I love you both but let's not ruin a nice night."

I feel like a jerk. "I'm sorry guys." Defeated, I get into the car and we head back to Lake Harmony.

Chapter Sixteen

Garrett

The next morning, my phone starts buzzing before I'm even out of bed. The only person it could be is my sister. I grab my phone off the nightstand. Sure enough, it's Julia. How much should I dread this?

Julia: Group Text (minus Hill)

Julia: Garrett- Jackson spilled the beans. You and Hill made a fake truce so we wouldn't ban you from social outings with all of us!!! How did you think that would work? Obviously, it didn't! case in point= LAST NIGHT!!! WTFFF!!!

Me: Sorry

Bree: Jiminy Crickets G! I love Hilly but she did you bad with this. Why didn't you guys just talk it out? Fix whatever is broken?

Me: Seriously Bree? I tried. She wouldn't even discuss it. She took control and it was her way or nothing.

Bree: Aw. Sorry big guy. She's a tough cookie. I knew something was fishy

Jackson: Everyone breathe and let Jules have her say

Rob: Oh! this should be fantastic!! Can't wait.

Cooper: ^^I'm kinda with Rob on this one^^

Noah: ^^Me too LOL^^

Me: Thanks assholes

Sam: Paul and I are sorry but this can't continue. Hill is stubborn but SO ARE YOU!!! What's the plan, Jules? We're here to help. How did Hill convince you to lie to all of us? Shame on you G. SHAME ON YOU!

Me: IT'S HILLARY!!!!! THAT IS ALL I HAVE TO SAY. SHE CAN BE MEAN

Ellen: OMG SO FUNNY. G scared of Hill. Scott and I will help too!

Stella: Ditto + Griff

Griff: Don't get me fired please *praying emoji hands* she is scary-agree with G man. I respect my balls and penis too much *praying emoji hands* Please remember I have to work closely with her "worried"

Julia: Ski Cabin Weekend-Change of Plans

Julia: Old Plan=Group weekend/ New Plan= Ditch + Fix

Me: Fuck

Rob: LMAO*high five hand emoji* ROTFLMAO *crying laughing emoji*

Jackson: Do not let Hillary find out about the change in plans or we are ALL dead. We may be dead afterward anyway, but let's hope at the end of this no blood has been shed- *nervous emoji*

Me: Great. Julia- just keep my safety in mind

Julia: Give me a break little brother. You were an Army Ranger in danger for most of your life and you are afraid of a woman?

Me: Hillary is no ordinary woman. She is feisty and knows how to use knives!!!

Griff: True- especially carving knives *scary eyes emoji*

Me: Thanx Griff

Griff: Sorry- I am scared *nervous emoji *

Bree: I'm with Jules on this. If we don't get Hill in a situation with you where she is forced to talk this through G she won't. Whatever happened – we probably don't want to know- is upsetting and she is hurt. When she is hurt, she gets into battle mode. Which is currently "Kill Garrett/Secret Truce Pact" …yes?

Me: Yes… Continue Jules

Jules: We all act like the game plan is our group weekend except it ends up being just the two of you. I won't go into details because you can be a bit in the unknown to save yourself a little bit-deal.

Noah: Oh I like that. Gives him a little bit of an "I wasn't in on the trickery"

Jackson: Yep.

Bree: Noah and I are out anyway because well…I'm preggers and can't ski and Noah was going to cover for Jackson at the practice.

Jackson: Thanks again Noah…if you want out I will be here now.
Noah: Nope all good. Enjoy the weekend off w Julia and the kids
Jackson: *thumbs up emoji*
Rob: For those of us stuck at home now- Sat nite-Coops? Beer and wings?
Ellen: We're in
Sam: Us too
Julia: Oh us too! Yay, fun.
Me: Please plan my funeral. What's the plan for getting to the cabin?
Julia: Same as before- Rob takes you up and I take Hill but we DITCH you!

Chapter Seventeen

Hillary

I'm so excited about this weekend. I love skiing. Zipping down a snow-covered mountain with the wind in my face is intoxicating. There aren't too many thrills I enjoy, but the freedom and escape I get from skiing, brings me such peace of mind it's hard to describe. Not to mention, having my friends with me to share drinks with at the end of the day. It's the best of both worlds.

Thankfully, the ski cabin is big enough to spread out, and, even though Garrett will be with us this weekend, there's enough space to not be near him if I don't have to be. I'm still so pissed at him from the concert. What the hell did he think? That just because I had a great buzz going I wasn't still pissed that he used me the last time I drank a little too much around him. Was he expecting the same result and the same invitation? Well, he had another thing coming if he did. I shut that down—and fast. I'm surprised no one said anything to me after that blowout. Maybe I wasn't as loud as I thought I was. Or they didn't catch on. Whatever. The bottom line is Garret Stone will never be someone that gets near me again.

I'm packed and ready to go. Julia is picking me up, and we'll start the drive to the cabin. Jackson and the guys will head up later. Jules and I will get everything ready for the rest of the gang when they start to arrive after the workday. Everyone should be there by bedtime.

I hear Julia honk, so I grab my gear and head out to her car.

"Hey, do you need any help grabbing your stuff?" she asks.

"That would be great. With my ski gear and my weekend bag, it will take me two trips. I also packed some food for snacks and some wine and booze for drinks," I say.

"You didn't have to do too much. You know everyone pitched in a few bucks, and I went to the store to get everything," Julia says.

"I know. But I had some leftovers from an event. It's nothing too exciting so don't get your panties in a bunch."

Julia laughs at me. "Fine, but I got enough for us to last the weekend and then some. You know me…the planner."

"Ah yes, Julia…the great planner. Come on let's get up there. I need some fresh air and some mountain snow. What time do you think the guys will show up?" I ask.

"Jackson said they would be up shortly after us. He'll finish work on time, then hitch a ride with my brothers. Fewer cars and gas to waste if they ride together. I think he's hoping they'll take Rob's truck with the snow."

"Probably a good idea just in case."

***

Two hours later, the cabin is ready and food is warming in the crock pot. Our first dinner will be casual for whoever wants to eat when they get here. I made beef stew with fresh bread and a green salad.

"Oh, Jackson just sent a text that the guys are almost here," Julia says. "Hmm…Jackson thinks I should run into town to fill up the tank. He said the temperature is going to drop and doesn't want the gas tank to be too low. Do you mind if I run and do that? Are you okay staying here alone?"

"Sure, go ahead. I'm a big girl. I'm just going to pour myself a drink and take my book and sit next to the fire. The best thing his parents did in this place was the electric fireplace. Turns on with just the push of a button. Love it!"

"Ok, be back soon," Julia says.

"No worries. Take your time."

***

After about twenty minutes I hear feet coming up the stairs on the outside deck and men laughing. Ah, the men must have arrived. I look over as the door opens and in walks Rob, Julia's younger brother, "Hey, how was your drive?"

"Good, I always get a little more worried the closer we get to the cabin looking for deer to jump out in front of me, but none tonight. Where's Jules?"

"She ran to fill up the gas tank since Jackson said temps are dropping."

"Oh good, that's not a bad idea. Hey Garrett, help me unload our shit from the truck so I can go do that too. Hill, do you need me to grab anything else while I run out? Do we have enough beer?"

"I think so. We brought two cases. How much do you think you are going to drink?"

"Well….dunno. Anything else? Whiskey?"

"No, I don't think we brought anything but beer and wine."

"Fuck, okay while I fill up the tank I will go run and grab some whiskey. I'd rather have it now than worry about it tomorrow. Sam and Ellen are right behind me, and Jackson is heading up with them."

"Oh, I thought he was coming up with the two of you?"

"Uh, nope. He got stuck at work a little longer and we left without him. Alrighty, I'm gonna get the truck emptied so I can fly and get gas and whiskey. Be right back."

Rob flies outside to help grab a load while Garrett stands there with his arms full of the first load, "Hill who's got what rooms? Where should I go with my things?"

"I think we planned to put you and Rob in the bunk room."

"Okay, that works. Let me go drop this back there and then I will help Rob grab whatever else he has. Guide him back here when he comes back in."

"Yep."

Rob pushes back through the door, "This is the last of the stuff other than ski gear, we can leave that in the truck for now. Where'd he go?"

"Bunk room."

"Cool." Rob wanders back toward the bunk room. I hear them talking in hushed tones so not loud enough that I can hear anything.

After a few minutes, they both wander back out. "Hey, I'm gonna go fill up and grab the booze. See you in a bit."

Garrett looks at Rob, "Do you want me to come with you?"

"Nah bro, Hilly won't bite. Will you Hilly? I will be right back. Damn, what's cooking? It smells heavenly in here."

"I made some beef stew for dinner. When you get back you can have some."

"Yum. Sounds like a plan. Later."

Rob winks at me and then turns to Garrett, "You sure you're good man?"

"Yeah."

Garrett and I are left alone just staring at each other. I lift my eyebrow at him, "Go do whatever. I'm going to sit here and relax with my wine and book until everyone else gets here. Do whatever you wish but preferably away from me."

"I'm going to grab a beer and check out the fire pit. See if we have any wood to burn out back."

"I'm sure we do. You know Jackson's parents never leave things half-assed."

He just grunts at me, turns, and stalks away. Yes, please just go away. I grab my book and keep reading.

***

I stop reading and look at my watch and realize it has been an hour since my best friend Julia left. Where the hell is she? I sent her a text message.

Me: Did you get lost?

I watch as I see bubbles. She is texting me back at least.

Julia: no
Me: Where are you?
Julia: Driving
Me: Where? You went to get GAS
Julia: I did get gas
Me: Why aren't you here?

I see bubbles again and then nothing.
Five minutes later still nothing.

Me: JULIA!!! WTF WHERE R U????
Julia: Driving home
Me: WHAT? WHY?
Julia: You lied. Fix it. Jackson will pick you up Sunday
Me: EXCUSE ME. WTF EXPLAIN
Julia: Truce Pact
Me: I'm going to kill him
Julia: Nope- it's all you Hill
Me: You are dead

My phone starts ringing. Oh, look, now my former best friend wants to talk to me. She drives me up to the woods, deserts me with my enemy, and now she wants to talk. Wait…does that mean Rob isn't coming back either? Is anyone else even coming? Oh, they are dead.

"HELLO."

"Before you get pissed and hang up I want you to take a deep breath and I want you to just listen. Can you do that Hillary?"

"Mhm."

"I love you; we all love you. We all love Garrett too. Obviously, something happened between the two of you that caused some very hurt feelings. I know you Hill and I can guess that it was something very personal that must have finally happened between the two of you. I am not asking for an explanation because it isn't my business and if you wanted to talk about it you would have by now. He has also respected you by not sharing the details of whatever has transpired. Honey, this can't continue. It isn't about this feud between the two of you. It's not. Does it suck that my brother and my best friend don't want to be in the same space together anymore when they used to be like best friends themselves, yes? BUT…what I am more concerned with is that you love, are hurting. You don't get this fierce and hostile if you aren't hurting deep inside and I hurt for you. Please, please fix this. Find a way to talk it through. Find common ground. If he did something wrong-which he probably did- make him own that mistake. Just talk it out. Figure out a way to stop hurting. I love you and I hate to watch you not be happy. Did we all finally gang up on you and leave you both stranded in the cabin with no vehicle to escape? Absolutely. Do we all love you guys and want to see you finally hash it out and figure out a way to honestly move past the hurt and not use some ridiculous fake truce pact? Again Yes. Blame me. Blame the gang. Don't blame Garrett as he is just as much a victim in this Ditch Pact as you are."

"Ditch Pact?"

"Yes, this current situation you have found yourselves in. We learned from the best."

"I hate you."

"No, you don't. Talk to him. Work it out. You have plenty of food and booze. Your ride will be there to get you both on Sunday. Love you. Bye."

"Fine. Bye."

I need a lot more wine stat. My asshole friends.

Chapter Eighteen

Garrett

Julia: She knows. Good luck. See you Sunday

Do I dare even go back inside? Ugh…that was their grand plan right. Ditch me here with her in the middle of the woods so she couldn't run away. Force her to talk things out with me. I should have brought some armor. May as well go face the enemy. I walk into the main room of the cabin and there is no Hillary.

I look and see the door to the room she is sleeping in is shut. It's now or never. I take a deep breath, man up, head towards the door and knock. "Hill, can we please talk."

"Go away."

"See that's the problem Hill. No matter what you want to do or not say to me we are stuck here together for the weekend. Sooner or later, you have to come out of that room and I will tell you this- if you try to avoid me I will find you. I will force you to hear me out. I will talk to you before Sunday comes and we will work through this shit."

"Fuck off."

This tactic isn't going to work with this woman.

"I will give you some cooling off time, but I will be back and in case you even think you can try to leave-you can't. I believe Rob took your coat and your purse when he left."

I hear her moving around the room and banging through the room, "FUCK! I hate all of you!"

"I'll be in the living room. If you get hungry come on out and eat with me."

This is going to be a long weekend. I head to the kitchen and grab a beer and sit back on the sectional by the fire. My phone went off and I reach to grab it.

Julia: Maybe this will help you remember...*pic* *pic* *pic* *pic* *pic*
Me: I skim through the pictures she sent-good memories -Thanks
Julia: Any luck?
Me: Negative
Julia: Keep trying

Looking through the five images that Jules sent me I remember the day each of them was taken. The first picture was of us kids growing up. Julia, Bree, Sam, Hillary, Rob, and I all squeezed together on the back deck stairs eating big slices of watermelon in the summer in our bathing suits. The next one was when we were a little older and the girls were at the lake as teenagers laying in the sun and I was handing Hillary an ice cream cone. The following was my high school graduation and Hillary had her arms around me squeezing me tight with tears in her eyes before I went to boot camp. Next was when I was able to come home in between for Julia's wedding and Hillary and I were paired up together at the wedding. Finally, the picture that's worth a million words from Memorial Day when shit hit the fan. It's a picture of the two of us laying out on one of our floating rafts in the lake after drinking all day snuggled up together most likely sleeping off all our beer consumed.

***

Flashback to Memorial Day- The Incident

The weather couldn't be more perfect -- sunny and eighty-two degrees outside. The lake water is still a bit cool for this early in the year, but it doesn't matter because we have the boats out on the lake and the rafts for the girls. The kids are taking turns tubing with Uncle Rob. Even Grandma and Grandpa have the pontoon boat out. When we have a big crowd, we camp the masses on Flynn Island and use the rafts for the ladies to float and get sun. It's easier to keep the coolers on the sand than in the boats. It's been a full weekend of drinking, boating, and laughing with everyone. I think everyone needed a weekend to relax and chill out. I know I did. I have been dealing with a bunch of rowdy senior boys this year and stupid pranks around town. It's going to be a long summer until they head off to college.

"Hey, who's up for a round of tubing Olympics," Rob asks.

"I'm in," Jackson shouts, "Jules, grab my son and your besties…let's do this!"

"Your son? Jackson," she laughs. "Is he not our son?"

"Come on, you know what I mean. I need to show him how it's done."

Rob punches Jackson in the arm, "How what's done, old man? How the elderly fall off the tube and get a water enema?"

"Oh, gross Uncle Rob," Daniel says. "Dad, should we bet on who can ride the tube the longest standing?"

"Oooh…game on little man," Rob says. "First Olympic competition will be about who can stand on the moving tube the longest?"

"Oh, dear god," Julia says. "Rob, just remember my husband has been drinking today and if he gets hurt, he is the medical doctor with us on the water today and we're screwed."

"No worries sis. Worst case we are a short ride to the hospital. Who's up first and who is competing? Get your asses on das boat."

Hillary, Jackson, Daniel, and I join Rob on the boat. "Anyone else," I ask as the rest of them head towards the island and look at us like we are crazy.

My dad laughs from his pontoon, "No kids, you have fun but if you need us, wave your arms around and I will drive the pontoon over to take away any casualties."

We head out into the water and Daniel decides to go first to set the bar high. He is going to prove to his dad that he can outlast his ability to stand on the tube. He last about a minute with the way Rob is driving the boat around.

"Are you trying to kill my son or are you going to drive like that with me too," Jackson asks.

"What? Are you scared? I was taking it easy. He's just a kid."

We spin around and grab Daniel and he is cracking up laughing as he climbs back into the ski boat. "How'd I do? That was hilarious."

"You were awesome! Lasted a whole minute," Hillary says. "Jackson, you're next."

We watch Jackson head into the water with a fancy dive and climb up on the tube and give a thumbs up. He lasts barely thirty seconds and falls on his face and comes up laughing. We spun around and pick him up.

"Jesus, I felt like a drunk sailor on that thing. I have no idea how the hell you lasted up there Daniel."

"Pure Strength and awesomeness."

At this point, we can hear the cackling coming from our family on the island and other boats. "Okay, I will go next. Not sure I can beat this kid, but I think I can beat Jackson." I jump in the water and swim over to the tube.

I am barely on the tube and standing and my jackass of a brother guns the boat and I go flying backward off the tube and into the water. I come out of the water and see Rob and Hillary give each other a high five. Assholes. I'm out. I swim back up to the boat. "Nice. Real nice you two."

Hillary stands up in her barely there itsy-bitsy bikini and puts on her life vest and smiles, "Okay boys, now let me show you how tubing Olympics is won." She looks over at Rob, "Be real Robbie, no trickery, I want to win for real." She heads over to the back of the boat and pulls the tube in with the rope and then climbs on without getting wet. "Daniel, sweetheart, hand Auntie Hill her beer please."

Daniel walks over and grabs her beer from her cup holder, and she sticks it in her life vest with a wink. "Okay, boys…nice and steady." She slowly sits back on her knees, and we all watch as Rob slowly starts to pull Hillary into a standing position then she pulls her beer out of her vest and is casually standing on her tube being pulled around the lake drinking and waving at everyone like Miss America.

***

Later that night I follow Hill home to make sure she gets in okay. We've all been drinking heavily all weekend. We've had a lot of sun, booze, and food but no matter what we've done my protective instincts are still in gear and we have a lot of summer timers in town.

She stumbles up onto her porch but can't get the key in the door. "Garrett, I don't think my key works. Can you break the door down? I really must pee."

"Give me your keys Hill. I will get you in your house." With a steady hand, it doesn't take much to unlock the door and she bursts past me and into her hall bath. I started dragging her lake bag and cooler into the house for her that she dropped outside the door. She walks into the kitchen still wearing her coverup but no bikini.

"Um Hill, where's your swimsuit?"

"Took it off because it was damp and gross."

"Do you want to change? Or put something on with more coverage maybe?

"Nah, I need to shower first."

"Do you want to go do that?"

"Nope. I'm hungry again. Want to have a snack?"

Fuck she is trying to kill me. "Sure. Do you still have that cowboy salsa or any of those sandwiches left?"

"OH, both…I didn't take them all and I have some spinach dip left in the fridge. I'll grab those and you grab more beers."

"Not sure we need more beer."

"Party pooper. You can walk home from here. What a great weekend! I wish it didn't have to end. Oh my god, this food taste so good. Why does the sun always make me so hungry? And horny?"

"Um, what?"

"That's true you know."

"What?"

"The sun makes me horny. Doesn't it make you horny?"

"I'm a guy Hill, anything makes a guy horny."

"Hmm, true."

"It's frustrating though. A perfect weekend like this and now I'm horny and well…no one to handle that for me. Except for Bob."

"Who the fuck is Bob?"

"Bob. You know. My battery-operated buddy."

Rubbing my hand over my face, "Jesus Hill, you are killing me right now."

"Why Garrett, what's the big deal? I happen to like sex. I enjoy a good orgasm. Why is that so hard to understand? The problem is I tend to attract losers. So, therefore, no orgasm, or no orgasms unless they are helped by Bob."

"Okay, I guess we are having this conversation."

"Yes, be a big girl and talk to me about this Garrett. It's not a big deal. You have sex. I have sex. You obviously won't have sex with anyone in this town because no one here is good enough for you but whatever. But you cannot tell me that you do not have sex. I mean look at you!"

"First of all, yes, I have sex Hill, but it has nothing to do with no one being good enough for me in Lake Harmony. I am the sheriff so that puts a little dilemma on me wanting to wine and dine the local ladies or have sex with anyone local. What happens if I have sex with someone here and it goes bad? That would make for a bad scene. I avoid anything weird happening or a bad reputation, so I head a town or two over and don't mix ladies with home."

"Are you some kind of man whore?"

"Hill, when do I have time to be a man whore? I am always with all of you or at work. I do date, but I don't have a girlfriend right now. Honestly, I am not sure if I want something long-term, or if I haven't found the right person yet. Don't know."

"Mmm." Hillary stares at me. "Why don't we sleep together?"

"What?" I say as I choke on my food.

"I trust you, you know me, and we both need someone to scratch an itch, sounds like a win-win to me."

"Hill you have no idea what the hell you are talking about."

"Come on, let's live a little. We aren't teenagers anymore. Let's kiss and see if we have chemistry. For all we know it will be like kissing my brother and gross. Trust me." She moves faster than expected and puts her arms around my head, leans in, and brushes her lips against me. She quickly pulls back with a quiet gasp and opens her eyes staring into mine. After a moment she smiles and then pushes in with a full attack on my mouth and body.

I know I should stop what's happening. We've both been drinking and probably aren't thinking straight, and it would be the right thing to do. But part of me thinks I'd be a fool to stop what I have always wanted. Her hands are all over me. I need to end this before it goes too far.

"I have wanted to do this for so long," Hillary says as her hands go to the button on my shorts, and she bites my earlobe. "Let's see what you've got sheriff now that you've caught me because I've been a very bad girl."

I snap, and all good judgment goes flying out the window as all my blood moves from my brain down to my cock. I have Hillary wanting me and I can't walk away. My dream girl is wanting me and so I'm going in. I grab her hands before she can grab my cock, "Bad girls don't get to make the rules. Let's be clear here Hill if you want this then you better know that anything that happens in the bedroom happens under my command, not yours. Do you hear me?"

"Yes, Sheriff."

***

Present

It's been about thirty minutes since I sat down, and I hear Hillary opening her room door and her coming out. She walks into the kitchen not looking at me, grabs a bowl of her beef stew, and another bottle of wine, and then goes back to her room and slams the door.

She just made her move and showed me how she plans on handling this situation-avoidance-as usual. Waiting for her isn't going to work. I also don't have forever because I know she has already gone through a bottle of wine if she grabbed a second. If I can't talk to her, maybe I can write to her? I got up and start looking for some paper around the house and a pen. Once I find that I grab another beer and sit back down. Time to lay out all my cards and hope for the best outcome. I take a big drink of my beer, scrub my hand over my face, and crack my neck. You'd think I'm going into battle and in one way I am.

Hill,
Since you won't come out and talk to me, I figured I would sit here and write you a letter. Maybe you will read it because it isn't a direct threat or maybe you will tear it up, but I am going to take the chance you will read it because I have nothing else left to try. Did you know I believe there's something magical about letters? I honestly believe that because for the years I was in the Rangers-especially in the years I was in not-so-safe deployments- your letters kept me alive. Seriously, that isn't a lie to bring you out of your room to talk to me. I'm being 100 percent honest with you. Do you know that you were one of the only people that continued to write to me over the years? It's true. It became easier once we always emailed but I still have every letter or card you ever wrote by hand to me. If you don't believe me, I will show them to you if you ever speak to me again. I miss you. I miss you terribly. I want you back in my life. How do we get there? How do we fix this?
I'm Sorry

I rip the paper off the tablet, fold it in half and knock on her door before I slide it under the door. *Up to you sweetheart. It's your move.* I sit back down and wait.

A few minutes later, the door opens and closes, but no comment. I get up to look and see my note lying on the floor. I get up and walk over and then realize that it isn't my note but a different one. She wrote me back.

Dear Sorry,
Those are sweet words about tough memories. What exactly are you sorry about? That you slept with me and ran! I'm sorry that I am such an embarrassment to you that you couldn't even have the decency to be there in the morning when I woke up after spending the night together. What the fuck Garrett! Who does that? Maybe I should be the one that's sorry. Sorry, that I ever thought you were a man that I should respect. You are just like all the others. I'm completely disappointed in the male gender.

Oh shit. I made a bigger mess of things than I thought. Here I thought she was pissed at me for taking advantage and she's pissed at me for being an insecure asshole. How do I fix this???

Dear Disappointed,
You should be very disappointed… in me. I fucked up Hill. I was so ashamed of myself after that night. Not for being with you but for feeling like I took advantage of a drunken situation. I have been in love with you since we were kids. I never acted on it because I thought you saw me as Julia's little brother. Then when we spent the night together and I woke up with you wrapped around me. I should have been so happy that I finally had the girl of my dreams but instead, the guilt sucked me under. I knew we had been drinking all

weekend. I wasn't sure how much of that was responsible for our night and I didn't want you to wake up with regrets, so I left. I left to spare YOU the embarrassment of having to ask me to leave. Under no circumstances did I leave because I didn't want you. I've always wanted you! I still want you even when you hate me. I am in love with you-did you read that? I. AM. IN. LOVE. WITH. YOU. HILLARY.

This is the toughest hand I've ever played but I'm all in. Now it's completely up to her to how this plays out. I fold the paper in half and lean forward with my elbows resting on my knees. I'm taking deep breaths with my head hanging low. I feel like I am going to be sick. This is crazy! I've put my life in danger in more extreme circumstances yet this time I know control is not in my hands. I take a deep breath, stand up and march over to her door, knock, push the letter under the door, and wait right there. My feet won't take me away. It's time to face the music and I just need an answer. I heard her move to the door and grab the letter. A few moments later the door opens quickly.

She's crying, "You love me?"

"Yeah Hill," I say as I look into her tear-filled eyes, "and I probably always will."

"Why didn't you ever say anything to me or make a move?"

I grab her hand, "Come on, let's go sit down and finally have that talk we needed to have months ago, okay? I think we need to clear the air and figure out where we go from here because I'm done fighting you Hill, I love you too much to not have you in my life, and now that you know I love you there are other things we need to talk about."

"Okay, but I think I better make some coffee."

Chapter Nineteen

Hillary

I'm in the kitchen making coffee because I was so pissed at my friends for ditching me at the cabin in the woods with Garrett that I drank a bottle of wine and now he tells me he loves me and wants to have a serious conversation when I'm half in the bag. Wonderful timing as always Hillary. Fuck. Me.

I glance over my shoulder and see he's just watching me move around the kitchen, "Hey Garrett, can you just ah… clarify for me one more time please um, how you feel about me just so I have it clear because I'm functioning on about four glasses of cabernet in about two hours, and intoxication levels are pretty good right now you know."

"To sum it up Hill, I told you that I am in love with you, and I have been for a long time. Once you have some coffee in you and you sober up, we are going to continue this conversation. Good?"

"Yeah…sure. Got you." *What the fuck is happening right now? Am I sleeping? Did I get drunk and pass out? Pinch my arm to check,* "Ow."

"You okay over there?"

"Yep." *Not sleeping.* "Give me a sec, coffee is almost done." I make a very strong cup of coffee and head over and sit down with one leg bent under the other facing Garrett on the couch. "I think I will let you start."

"First, I want to tell you that I am sorry I hurt you by leaving that morning. That wasn't my intention. I woke up that morning and felt like I won the lottery. I had you all wrapped around me, snuggled up tight after making you come all night. It was like a dream come true for me. Then I thought about how much we had been drinking and how you told me how horny you were from the sun and how we could scratch each other's itch. I thought I had taken advantage of the situation. Honestly, I had no intention of letting it get that far but once you latched onto my ear and grabbed my cock my body took control of my actions. I left the way I did because I felt like I took advantage of you, and I was ashamed of myself. I have always tried to protect you from all those losers that you always found online and dated and right then I wasn't any better than any of those losers. I wanted to make sure when you woke up you didn't feel bad or feel uncomfortable that I was still there. I figured we'd talk about it later but then you avoided my texts and wouldn't talk to me for weeks. Then you just avoided me as much as possible and things got completely shitty from there. I am sorry. I didn't mean to hurt you. Can you please forgive me?"

Wow. I read that entire situation wrong, didn't I? I figured it was a smash-and-dash lady's night for him when instead he thought that's what I wanted or didn't want. This is so messed up. Why are we so stupid and stubborn?

"Um, wow. How fucking stupid is this!" I'm just shaking my head back and forth. He drops his head down.

"I'm so sorry Hilly. I didn't mean to hurt you."

"Enough Garrett!" Maybe that came out a little harsher than intended but the entire bottle of wine has me off kilter and now dealing with this news. His head pops up and he looks at me with those same eyes as when he was little. *I have broken this big bad man that has kicked more bad guy ass than GI Joe. Jesus Hillary. What the fuck have you done?*

"I think what we have here is a huge misunderstanding. When I woke up that morning, after the night we shared I thought wow, finally a guy I know and trust that I have a strong connection with both mentally and physically, and then poof you are nowhere to be found. It was like a dagger to the heart. I thought you were embarrassed that we had ended up in bed together. That you ran like a bat out of hell out of my bed so no one would ever know that we had slept together. I think that is what hurt me the most. Why I felt so hurt, used, and then so hateful."

His lips begin to lift into a smile, "So Hill, what you are saying is that if we would have talked earlier like I wanted to we would have solved this problem sooner?"

I look at him and say nothing for a moment, "You should probably quit talking while you are ahead Garrett. We talked now, and we cleared the air, so let's just move forward, shall we? Huh? You know I don't fight fairly so let's continue this conversation in the right direction. So, now what?"

He takes my hand that isn't holding my hot coffee, "How do you feel Hill? I told you how I feel about you. I understand that doesn't mean that your feelings match mine. I'm okay if they don't, but if there is a chance that you want to see if there could be something between us, I'd like to take that risk."

"Risk?"

"With you Hill, it's a risk."

"Very funny. Can I think about it?" Come on—I can't let him off that easy. It just wouldn't be right if I did. His face right now is killing me. He is dumbfounded that I honestly asked that.

"I'll give you time, but not much."

I start to smile and laugh, "Game on Garrett."

He puts my coffee down on the table, leans forward, pulls me into his arms, and kisses me. "I see this thing between us will never be easy, will it?"

"What fun would that be for either of us? There is something that I need to ask you about before we move ahead with this plan. I need another pact."

"Oh, Jesus, Hill—what now?"

"Our asshole friends brought the two of us out to a cabin in the woods for a weekend and ditched us here with no way to escape knowing that we were at odds. The only thing they have going in their favor is the food and alcohol here. They don't have any idea if this plan of theirs is going to work or not. By the way whose brilliant idea was this? Julia's? It was her idea, wasn't it?"

"Yeah, Julia figured out we were lying to everyone. She kind of cornered me about it but I didn't know all the details about the weekend. I did know she was ditching us here and I went along with it because I wanted to clear the air with you but that's about all I knew."

"Uh huh, whatever…anyway, they deserve to suffer a little bit and we deserve some time to figure out what this is without them interfering as they do."

"I agree with both to a certain extent because your paybacks can be a bit extreme, so I have to agree to them before I agree to the pact, and this time, I mean it."

"We will make The Solo Pact-they have to pick a friend. It's one or the other but not both."

"What? They must take sides?"

"Oh no, that's ridiculous. We aren't going to make it that simple. We both want to stay friends with all of them. We are going to act like this is a divorce and they must pick and choose who is going to do what and when and we are going to rotate the times we are available to be with them. We are going to be totally on board with this and drive them fucking crazy. Sometimes we will be available and sometimes neither of us is available because of course the two of us will be off secretly dating or - you know. It is going to be awesome and hilarious. The best part is we will have time to figure out if this thing between us is something worth fighting for since we already put all the fighting into it and if not, they won't suffer more. If we decide that our friendship turns into an amazing love story, then we let them in on our secret—eventually."

"You are so hot when you are creating secret missions."

"Then agree to my terms so you can take me in the bedroom and close the deal."

"You know I can't say no to you, now let's go back to your bed so I can make sure I remember what every inch of you tastes like. We only have about forty hours before someone shows up to see if we have killed each other or not."

Chapter Twenty

Hillary

I wake up to kisses on my shoulder and something hard resting against my butt. "Is that a banana in your pocket or are you happy to see me?"

Garrett leans into my ear, "More like a huge zucchini if we are talking fruit and vegetables. Morning."

"Morning. Do you realize this is our first morning together of our Solo Pact?"

"Yes, so what should we do to make it special?"

"I have some ideas of what you can do with your zucchini."

"Me too."

Garrett begins to kiss his way down my shoulder, and spine and then rolls me to my back and moves between my legs. "First, I need to make sure I remember how sweet you taste."

"Don't act like I'm going to stop you. Go check and do a very thorough job because if you don't, you may have to double-check your initial work."

I hear him chuckle before he blows a warm breath across my sensitive skin. Yes, sensitive because he made sure to make up for lost time and reexamine my entire body because he couldn't remember it well enough last night. If he gave us a few hours of sleep last night I'd be surprised. *Am I complaining? Hell no.*

This man knows how to throw me into an orgasm without much effort and he already has my breath hitching and my back curving off the mattress, "Do not stop. If you even…*oh my god*…think…*ohhh*…about it...kill you." My orgasm hits me so quickly and he continues to lick, suck, and nip me until every last spasm leaves me in a state of awe.

"I love the noises you make when you come Hill and how you for once just let yourself go. It's hot. He kisses me and I can taste myself, he moves down and licks around my nipple and blows warm air across making it pebble hard. Then moves to the other side and does the same.

"Garrett?"

"Hmm?"

"Put your big cock in my pussy now and fuck me or I'm going to bite you."

He leans back with a grin, "Hill, you know I will always make sure you do not leave my bed unsatisfied. How about this…I will even let you take the lead."

He grabs me and rolls, and I'm now laying on top of him. He gives me a kiss and a hard smack on the ass.

"Now get your pussy on my cock and ride me hard. I want to see your tits in my mouth but don't you dare come until I tell you to."

"Oh, now this I like. I do like to ride you like a bucking bronco. Give me all you've got, big boy. Let's see who breaks first."

***

After that last round of amazing orgasms, my stomach is telling me if I don't get up and eat something I could die. Garrett is dozing next to me, so I quietly slip out of bed and head toward the bathroom.

"Where do you think you are going?"

"Bathroom, shower, then food."

"That is a beautiful sight."

I stop and peer over my shoulder, "What? Am I walking funny after having your big cock ramming me all night and morning?"

"No, but I am admiring my handprints across your ass. Marked you mine. No takebacks Hilly."

I stop to catch my breath, "No takebacks. You have two minutes to rest and then you best be in that shower washing my backside you claimed as yours."

110

"I'd be happy to sweetheart. I'll give you a minute first."

"Thank you."

I continue to the bathroom and quickly use the toilet before Garrett comes in, although, no. I turn the shower on to warm the water and step in. I've barely put my head under the water to rinse off when I hear him come join me. He wraps his arms around me and gives me a tender kiss.

"Turn around, let me wash your hair." He takes my shampoo and pours some into his hands and smells it. "I love this stuff. You always smell like green apples. Makes me smile every time I smell this scent."

"I didn't realize that you noticed things like that."

He grabs my chin and tilts my face so I can look at him, "I notice everything about you Hill. Everything."

His big strong hands are washing my hair and massaging my scalp and it feels amazing. "Oh my god, can you do this every morning?"

"Well, I can do it every morning we spend together."

I open my eyes and look at him, "Really?"

"Really. If you let me in, I will spoil you rotten until my last breath Hillary. I told you that I love you. There isn't anything that I wouldn't do for you. Wait! Within reason and legal."

"Okay. Can I wash you too?"

"You can do whatever you want to me. I'm all yours. Now rinse. You can wash me after I put the conditioner in your hair."

"Sometimes I love that you grew up around all of us girls. You make a pretty good partner."

He rinses my hair and thoroughly makes sure the soap is out then squeezes the extra water out before applying the conditioner to my hair.

"My turn, can I use my apple stuff, or do you need your manly man shampoo?"

"I'm good. I don't mind smelling like you," he says with a big grin on his face.

I take the shampoo and give him a nice scalp massage along with his neck and while he just relaxes and lets me scrub his head, I have the chance to study his face. This is the relaxed face of the boy I've known my whole life. The boy that turned into a man, then a soldier, who now says he loves me. I've loved him my whole life too, but can I allow myself to drop the last of my guard and let him completely in-- I hope so. "Rinse."

"Oh man, that was awesome. Showers are a must-do together. I am so relaxed now. Let me soap you up now before the final rinse. I hear your stomach and it is about to eat me alive."

"Wait, let me soap you up first, and then you can do me."

"I think we need to put that on hold until I have fed you, babe."

"That's what I meant Garrett. Me soap you up and then you can soap me and rinse and done and done-you can do me again later after food."

***

After a late breakfast or early lunch, the two of us are laying on the couch snuggling together in front of the fire. We are both tired after having sex all night but not tired enough to go nap and miss out on our alone time. We don't want to be without each other right now, which is nice.

"Can I ask you something? You don't talk much about your time as a ranger in the army and I understand, but do you miss it?"

"I miss my team, and the family I made but I don't miss the danger or making everyone worry about me. It was a good career choice for me. I knew I needed to make a difference and then once I was in and 9-11 happened it just made that need to be there and fight for what was right so much bigger. I had people I loved to keep safe and a country to protect. I didn't realize that coming home and adjusting back to civilian life was going to be as difficult as it was, but I was lucky. Luckier than some because I was alive, healthy, I had my family, my friends, and local veteran groups for support."

"Why did you become Sheriff for Lake Harmony instead of just becoming part of Stone Builders and helping Rob take over for your dad? Wasn't that what your plan was going to be? I know you and Rob started picking up the rentals and flips once you were retired but then suddenly you were gone again off to the police academy."

"I tried but it just wasn't working. I was home for about a month when my dad pulled me out on the fishing boat and told me he was worried about me. He saw that I wasn't happy becoming part of the company and the noise was a trigger on building sites sometimes. He was friends with Tom Benson, the former Sheriff. They were buddies and Tom asked how I was transitioning back into civilian life and Dad told him he didn't think I was. Tom was the one that suggested I speak to someone about what it would take to become a policeman. I wasn't sure I wanted to go back in that direction, so I took a week and hung out with Tom and shadowed him at the station and on calls. Then I realized it may give me enough of my old life to balance out my new life. I went to the police academy and did what I needed to do and became a police officer. What I didn't know at the time was that Tom was sick. He told my dad but asked him not to tell me. He wanted the choice to be left to me, but he planned to get me in as a cop and then fill his shoes as the sheriff. Once he started his cancer treatments I was nominated and took over as Interim Sherriff and then when Tom got too sick to return, I got voted in as full-time Sheriff."

"Are you happy now Garrett? Have you found that balance that you needed?"

"I have, finally, but it wasn't an instant fix. Being able to protect the people I care about and the town that is important to me gave me back some of that purpose I guess I needed. Lake Harmony has a large community of veterans. Between Sam and Paul hiring veterans to work their programs at the nursery, my dad hiring a lot to be on his building crews and me getting Cooper here after his retirement makes a good balance for me. Coop is my brother from another time and having him here helps. It's hard because I can't talk about what I did, or where I've been, but with Coop—he's been in many of the same special op's situations. Knowing that I have him, and he understands is something, not even my brother Rob can offer me. Unless you've been in the service and those situations of war it's too hard to even comprehend. Sometimes I have trouble dealing with some of the shit I saw."

"I was so scared not knowing where you were and what you were doing but knowing it was most likely dangerous. There were times when ignorance was bliss ya know? Not knowing made it okay for me to get up and go to work and then complain about being tired without feeling guilty. God, that sounds like such an asshole thing to say, but it's true. There were so many times that I would think of you and send a little prayer up to whoever was looking out for you to keep you safe another day and please bring you home in one piece. Jules and Bree would cry together sometimes. She would be so upset and just need a moment to worry and not be judged. I couldn't. I just couldn't support her during those times because my heart wouldn't survive it. I had to be a bitch and avoid those times because…"

"Hey, come here. Aw, babe don't cry. I'm here and I'm in one piece so whomever you asked to watch over me heard you."

"It was so hard. Every time you came home on a short leave and then left again, oh my god Garrett, we all just turned into these zombies and forced ourselves to be normal. We were so proud of you and what you were doing but we were so scared to lose you. I remember when Jules found out you were done. That you were finally coming home. We all got drunk that night. The kids went to sleepovers and all of us went to your parents and made a fire. It was like the night of your graduation before you left us for boot camp. We all got so drunk your dad made us all sleep at your parents' and started collecting our car keys.

Even your parents got drunk. We were all just relieved to hear you were safe and heading home."

"I never knew that. Wow, I know that families have a lot to deal with when their family members are in the service, and I didn't make it easy because I knew that night at my graduation bonfire that I was planning on special ops of some sort. I wanted to push myself as far as I could, and I never really thought about the added danger and what that extra danger would mean to all of you. I'm sorry."

"I'm proud of you but I am so damn glad that you came home to us safely. Just promise you won't put yourself in crazy danger again. Sheriff danger I can handle but nothing like special ops stuff again. I couldn't survive that again."

"I promise. Those days are in my past and right now Hill, I am focused on the present and the future."

"Good answer. What do you want me to make for dinner tonight? We have some steak that Jules brought. Do you think you can go heat the grill in a bit and I'll whip up some food?"

"How about we make dinner together? I like to cook but I think having you in the kitchen will make me love to cook."

"Look at you, Mr. Smooth Talker. Deal. I need some protein to fill my reserves before I take you back to bed. We need to organize our plan a little bit before whichever shithead comes to pick us up tomorrow."

"I bet Jules sends one of the guys. She won't dare face both of us tomorrow in case things went south."

I look over at him with a devilish smile, "Oh she better be very cautious right now. She has absolutely no idea what kind of hornet's nest she just poked."

"What's the plan boss?"

"I think I can get used to you calling me boss lady."

"No, the boss part refers to this Solo Pact situation I seem to have gotten myself into again. I haven't heard the details, so you better start to explain while we make dinner before I agree to anything specific."

"Oh, look at you thinking you still have a choice. You are so adorable. I love that you are so good-looking and still think you are in charge."

"Enough Hill, start talking and I'll listen with a very open mind."

***

After dinner, Hillary sends a group text message to everyone while I sit back enjoying my beer and laughing.

Hillary: OK fuckers. All is good here. Really. Garrett and I have made the time to talk and really work through our differences this time although both of us -ME- I am very angry with all of you because as much as I enjoy the cabin my heart was set on flying down the snowy slopes with the wind in my hair. What I got was a weekend in a cabin with Garrett, to whom I wasn't speaking. As I said, all is forgiven, and we have moved past our differences and are in a good place. To discuss your actions from this little "Ditch Pact" and how it has worked out we (G and I) invite you all to a mandatory pizza-making dinner at the shop at 6 pm tomorrow. Since we have all this fucking pizza-making food here at the cabin—we may as well cook it up in my industrial ovens. Shame on all of you!
Garrett: No lie-all good and we will see someone tomorrow? Who's picking us up and what time?
Jackson: I will be there around noon for the both of you. I've been given the job of making sure this is a legit truce this time.
Garrett: It is- we will discuss it all tomorrow.

116

Chapter Twenty-One

Garrett

In the morning we lay snuggled up to each other, "We have a plan in place for our idiot friends but how are we going to manage this Hill? How are we going to continue being together? Do you have a plan for that? I may have an idea but figured I would check with you first."

"Lovely. Well, for one we need code names. If you text me or vice versa and we are with one of our idiot friends, they will be curious as to why we are texting during our Solo Pact, so we need code names."

"Probably a good idea. What should my code name be?"

"Oh, I already have yours, you are Hank, my service man."

"What!" Laughing, "Why am I Hank your serviceman?"

She rolls into me and sucks on my earlobe, "Because you are SO good at servicing my every sexy need."

"True. I've figured out how to read your body pretty well and given you amazing orgasms, haven't I? I accept. Then I know what your name should be."

"Yeah? Don't give me a hooker name please."

"No, you're no hooker but you are MY smitten kitten." I should be afraid, but she starts laughing. This is the silly girl I fell in love with as a teenager and her loud as hell makes no excuses, obnoxious laughter that she can't control without tears falling.

"Oh, my god. I am going to allow you to keep that because I can already think about a few ways you are going to regret that decision."

"Nah, never."

"Mmhm. Keep me posted on that Hank."

"So, code names-- check. I was thinking about the how, or the where. We can't be found at each other's places, so I was thinking I'd rent out one of our rentals. Rob won't know if someone is renting or not because I do the books and keep an eye on things. We have the new one we just flipped into a rental, and we haven't put it on the schedule yet. I can say I got a long-term renter that wants to come to write their novel. Not be interrupted. We will have a nice view of the lake, and fire pit thanks to the guys and I just put a hot tub in. It also has a two-car garage so we can hide our cars from anyone driving by just in case. How's that sound?"

"That sounds like the perfect love shack. I'm in!"

"Hill, I want to date you too though. As much as I love having you naked in my bed, I want to date you. I want to take you out and show you off. Since we can't do that here we have to be creative, but I think we can go into the city or go a few towns over. If we are going to take the time to make this work, we need to make sure to put in every effort."

"I love that G. I agree. We can do dates to the city and depending on our schedules we don't have to just do weekends. Maybe we can even coordinate our days off better. You have days during the week that you can switch, right? I have days during the week that are just office days so I can just say I'm doing that from home. Griff doesn't come in if he doesn't have an event to host for me, so he won't know if I am in or not and my clients are appointment only."

"So, when we get home later, I will snag the keys for the rental and when we meet at your shop to make pizzas and harass our friends with this crazy plan, I will give you the key and the garage opener for the rental. We need to keep it hidden though so we have time to explore this without too much input from everyone else."

"Okay, but hey…when are we meeting at the love shack?"

"As soon as we ditch our idiot friends tonight and can sneak over. Is that soon enough for you?"

"No, but I'll manage. I guess we better strip the beds and get this place ready before we head out. Jackson will be here in a bit."

"I'm so glad those assholes ditched us up here this weekend because if I had to go another day without you, I was going to lose my mind Hill."

"Well, they can't know they did something good Garrett, so you better be ready to knock them off their high horses later."

"For you baby, I will make them suffer. I'm looking forward to how you discuss the logistics with all of them and screwing with them about how I think this is the best approach. They honestly have no idea what shitstorm they are about to walk into and it's going to be so fun to mess with them just for a little while."

Chapter Twenty-Two

Hillary

After an awkward but hilariously fun ride home making poor Jackson our first victim of the plan, I am already at the shop organizing my thoughts and preparing the working kitchen for everyone to arrive and make pizza.

Jackson had drawn the short stick and had to come to pick up both Garrett and me from the cabin and drive us both back to Lake Harmony. We were both civil but wouldn't share with him what happened, what we talked about, or how things were other than we made peace and would share details with everyone tonight at dinner. He kept trying to ask, we kept avoiding answers.

Garrett was texting me from the front seat about all the dirty things that he was planning on doing to me as soon as the confrontation was over tonight. By the time poor Jackson dropped me off at home I was about to combust I was so turned on by his texts. Thankfully, I had enough time to unpack, calm down, and clean myself up a little. Knowing that I was getting naked again with Garrett I wanted to make sure he had something fun for him to enjoy under my jeans and sweater later.

I'm just writing out the Solo Pact details on my Whiteboard of Knowledge in the back when I hear someone come in. "Hill you back there," Garrett calls.

"Yep, come on back, just preparing for the talk."

He comes through from the hallway and smiles at me, "Anyone else here yet?"

"No, but they are expected shortly so don't get any ideas. After that car ride home and all those dirty texts I need you to just stay about two feet from my body right now."

"Oh yeah…or?"

"Not now Garrett. Let's focus. Come closer though and help me with these details later I will let you get naughty."

He walks over and starts laughing, "What's all this?"

"This is the Whiteboard of Knowledge, and she comes out whenever we need to brainstorm as a group or go over very important details. This is where we are laying out all the ground rules of the Solo Pact. How's it look?"

Solo Pact- Better NOT Together

Agreement between Hillary and Garrett-and friends- to share time equally but separately to avoid negative feelings and hostility while we take time to heal.

1. *Take Turns-One or the Other -AT ALL TIMES*
2. *Group Texts are still allowed*
3. *Important events (Birthdays, Weddings, Babies, Etc.) We will coordinate the time of the event and split the time equally with all of you.*

"Looks good to me," he says. "So, you are going to go over the rules here and I am going to be completely on board, exaggerate with you on examples of how this will work, promise that we have just agreed to go our separate ways for now because we are grown adults and can handle this respectfully, then I should avoid you at all costs within the room tonight to prove how this is going to work?"

"Exactly."

"You know, you can be quite scary when you want to be. I'm just glad that I secretly know that in a few hours, I am going to have you naked in my bed screaming my name."

"Okay, now you need to be good, but you can't be close to me when they start shuffling in. Try to stay on the opposite side of the room as me until we roll this baby out and show them the rules. First, I going to make them sweat a bit by ditching us at the cabin."

"Here, take this key and remote for the garage. The address is on the key chain. I think you know the house. You helped Sam with some of the landscaping."

"I know exactly where this is. Nice. The love shack baby. Oh, shh here they come."

***

Garrett and I make sure we are circulating the room at opposite ends and making small talk with our friends but still not discussing any details or answering any questions. We all work around the room making our personal pizzas. Everyone's eyes keep moving from him back to me and they are all trying hard to read the room and the mood, but we aren't giving them a clue. We finish making our pizzas and once they are put into the ovens, I ask everyone to have a seat.

"Thank you for coming even though I should be very angry with all of you. Who thought that putting two angry people in the same place without an escape plan was a smart idea? HUH?"

Julia is attempting to look brave but isn't quite hitting the mark. I stare at her until she cowers. "I just wanted to get you both in a situation where you couldn't avoid the problem. Hill, you tend to avoid things that you don't like and this was just something I had to do. You are my best friend, and he is my brother." She looks around for support and everyone is nodding along with her. "We all just wanted things back to normal. Is that too much to ask?"

"Yes, by forcing us and not giving us a choice in the matter. That wasn't very nice of you. What would have happened if you made it worse?"

"But we didn't, you said you talked and made amends," Julia adds.

"I said we talked things through yes, and we made peace with whatever happened." I look slowly at all our friends around the room—showing no emotion. "But... I don't think any of you are going to like where Garrett and I have ended."

Julia sits up straight, "What do you mean where you ended? I'm hoping to be friends again or more. Where else?"

"As I said, I don't think you are going to like where Garrett and I ended up, but this doesn't concern any of you,

123

it doesn't, it's about the two of us. We consider your feelings, and of course, we do because you are our best friends, so when discussing our next steps, we did keep that in mind. Well, maybe it's just easier if the two of us explain this together. Garrett, can you come here and help me explain this to them."

The two of us roll my Whiteboard of Knowledge into the room but they still can't see what's written on the other side.

Rob says, "Oh shit, the whiteboard. She means business."

I stop and turn to face him, "Yes, I do Rob. Thank you. Now, Garrett and I had a lot of time to talk and go over the details of how we think this can work so that no one is feeling left out." I slowly turn the whiteboard around so that the writing is facing our friends.

"What the fuck is a Solo Pact Hillary? Are you in another fake truce again," Julia asks.

Garrett raises his hand towards her, "Jules, just give us a minute to explain. You kind of forced our hand here by ditching us at the cabin. I want all of you to know that I appreciate you wanting us to smooth things over and we have. We've figured out a way to co-exist for now. No, this is not a fake truce again. We talked about what was bothering Hillary, and we did have a major miscommunication between the two of us and we worked our way through that, but we also realized that the damage has been done. We want to just ask all of you now to support us and let us heal. Is this going to be how things are forever? No, but this is how Hillary and I need them to be for now."

"Thank you, Garrett, well said. So, the Solo Pact is just that. We will both be your friend but not at the same time."

Noah asks, "Is this like a divorce, and we pick sides? Because guys I've been through that before, and it doesn't end well for anyone. Even if you don't pick a side there is always a divide."

"No, Hillary and I have a very clear understanding of how this will work. Hillary, maybe we should give some examples?"

"Good idea Garrett. Let's say next weekend Noah, you, and Bree want to have a BBQ and invite us all over. Either Garrett or I will attend, but not both of us."

Bree raises her hand, "Fiddlesticks, so how do we know whom to ask?"

"Easy, we will sort of volley the invites. If Garrett is off duty and can attend, he goes, if I don't have an event I go. If we are both free one of us will decline the invitation."

"So, we can just invite both of you and, then the two of you will figure it out," Jackson asks.

"It will be best to do that in the beginning, yes, until we determine a - *who's turn is it* -system. Then everyone will just keep track. Obviously, it will only become an issue when we would do group things."

"Obviously," Garrett adds shaking his head in understanding.

"G man, you are okay with this. It's not just Hillary telling you what she wants you to do again is it," Jackson asks.

"Man, I know. I went along with the fake truce but that was because Hillary wouldn't talk to me. I needed her to listen to me and hear me out. With Julia's cabin ditch plan, we had the time to sit and talk and clear the air. We both know exactly where we are and what expectations we have from each other. Right Hill?"

"Yes, we are very clear on the details of this. You all pushed us to make up and we thank you for it, but our feelings were hurt and now we just need time apart to heal and forgive. I don't know if that will be a long time or maybe never, but you all owe it to us to give us the privacy and time to figure it out. Don't you think?"

"This sounds ridiculous to me. Are you guys serious right now," Rob asks.

"Totally serious, bro. As a matter of fact, as soon as my pizza is done, I'm leaving since this is her place. I told

Hillary I would be here to support her when we told you all how this is going to need to be for now for us to move forward. I hope you will respect our wishes. I care about Hillary, and if you care about us you will do this for us."

"I wish that things could just go back to the way they were before whatever happened," Julia says with defeat.

"Jules, it will all work itself out. We just need time. Hillary, do you have a box for my pizza so I can let you have tonight with the gang?"

"That is very nice of you Garrett. Yes, they are in the back but you will have to help me grab some for everyone else."

The two of us calmly walk to the back stock room area and Garrett keeps a dialogue going about how he is so happy that we finally got the air cleared and he wishes me nothing but happiness just in case they are listening which I'm sure they are. He won't stand in my way, and we will figure out how to share our group time without any problems. As I am grabbing the box off the top shelf I feel his hands sliding up my legs and then he pinches my ass. I turn and give him a dirty look but he just winks.

"I think it's best that you leave now. Let's go get your pizza."

We both head back into the kitchen and they are all watching with their eyes big and waiting for us to tell them that we are kidding. No, sorry but you assholes are going to suffer a little bit now while Garrett and I figure out what is happening between us, and just for interfering, we aren't going to let you in on our little secret.

"See you later guys. Enjoy your pizza," Garrett says as he heads out the door.

I turn towards all my friends and clap, "Any other questions? If not, let's get our pizzas and enjoy our dinners." I watch as all my friends don't dare say another word. They keep glancing at each other, their food, and the words written on the Whiteboard of Knowledge. *God, I am loving this so far!*

Chapter Twenty-Three

Garrett

I hear the garage door go up so Hillary must have finally gotten rid of our friends, cleaned up the shop, and got away. While waiting for her I made a fire and brought over a throw blanket, made the master bedroom up, and even made sure to have some shampoo and soap in the shower.

"Where are you Hanky baby?"

"In here my little Smitten Kitten. How did things go with the gang after I left?" I watch as she walks into the room and if I'm not mistaken, she seems a little hesitant. "Come here," I pat the couch next to me.

She chuckles, "They don't know what to think. They are still wondering if we are pulling their leg or if this is legit. I can't wait until one of them invites us over. I think everyone is planning on trivia night at Coop's Tuesday so that will be our first group challenge. I am so excited to mess with them. Thank you for being such a team player '*We need time to heal*' was a fabulous addition to our Solo Pact."

"I wanted to help sell it and we do need time together without their two cents and interruptions. Agreeing with you about everything helped convince them I think. Julia and Jackson have always seen how I feel about you and they were pushing me to tell you but I didn't want to stir up trouble, so I added in just enough to show them that we finally talked about what most likely happened between us, how I feel about you and that you don't feel the same about me. For all they know I do need to heal my broken heart that you stomped all over."

"At this point, I don't care what it takes as long as we have time to ourselves, have time to date, and see how we are as a couple, and I get to play with your naked bits."

"You can always play with my naked bits. Come on, let me show you the house. Do you want to sit outside in the hot tub and look at the stars with me?"

"I didn't bring a suit."

"Did I forget to tell you that this is a clothing-optional love shack?"

"You might have forgotten to mention that, but I am one hundred percent on board with that plan. Show me the bedroom and then help me get naked."

***

After undressing each other and getting a good taste of Hillary we are relaxing in the hot tub under a night sky full of stars. She's relaxing against me, and I have my arms around her.

"Did you think that we'd ever be here together in this situation Garrett?"

"I had hoped one day we would find our way to each other."

"I'm not sure that I thought you and I would ever be a couple but what I do realize now is that you were my standard. I held all the guys I met and dated up against you, but they never came close. Not even a little bit. Maybe that was my heart telling me it may have already belonged to you?"

"Maybe? I don't know. I hated watching you bring all those guys into Coop's place on your dates. Julia would always happen to mention you had a new date or Coop would text me to come in and have a beer."

"I wondered how you always seemed to appear when I had those dates. I'd look over and sure enough, there you were having a beer on your seat at the end of the bar talking to Cooper."

"If you knew that I would always show up, why did you always have your dates there?"

"I knew that no matter what you had my back. If you weren't there, I knew Coop had my back on your behalf. I never put myself into a situation I couldn't handle but it was nice knowing I had two trained killers to protect me."

"Coop knew that if you were there with a guy to keep an eye on your table. He watched out for you even without having to ask because he knew you were special to me. I'm sure he will question this solo pact and I'm not sure if I can lie to Cooper. We have an understanding, but he knows not to spill the beans. I won't offer the truth unless he comes right out and asks. Deal?"

"I'm okay with that. It's not like anyone can torture that information out of Cooper."

"It's getting late baby, do you want to go home, or should we stay here tonight?"

"If you don't mind, I'd like to sleep here tonight and wrap myself up in you. This is too new to not enjoy as much as possible right now. I'm still a little worried that when I wake up it may not be real. I am happy right now G, and it's been a long time since I think I've felt this content and I want to enjoy the butterflies as long as possible."

"That sounds perfect to me. Come on, let's dry off and slide into bed. We didn't get much sleep over the weekend and we both have an early morning."

We dry off and walk into the house hand in hand. "I'm going to grab a glass of water; do you want one?"

"Yes, please."

"Okay baby, go ahead and get ready for bed. I'll be there in a second. I want to make sure we are locked up."

I walk around the house making sure the garage door is down, and the back door is locked, and get two glasses of water. By the time I make it back to the bedroom, Hillary is curled up under the covers and sound asleep. I put a glass on her side table and then gently slid into bed next to her. "Night sweetheart."

Chapter Twenty-Four

Garrett

Mondays are always a tough day at work. There seems to be chaos that has happened over the weekend and things to sort out but since I took the weekend off there seems to be more to deal with than usual. For lunch, I headed over to the 1-Stop General Store for a sub sandwich and some of Gertie's potato salad.

I'm standing at the deli counter waiting for Gertie to come back out and whistling a tune. Trying to decide do I want roast beef or turkey today.

"Seems our Sheriff is in a very good mood today," Gertie says. "You must have had a very good weekend! For a Monday I wouldn't expect to see you in here whistling and smiling like that if there wasn't a good reason."

"Now Gertie, don't go reading into too much. I had a good weekend is all and there aren't too many things to worry about waiting for me back at the station."

"Either way Sheriff, it is nice to see you having a good day—whatever it may be about. What can I get you today? I just made a fresh batch of my potato salad. You want that with your roast beef or turkey sub today?"

"Am I that predictable?"

"With your lunch order? Yes."

"How about this, I'll let you decide."

"In a good mood and accommodating. Interesting indeed. Let me get your lunch for you so you can get back."

"Thanks, Gertie, I appreciate it." I feel my phone go off and grab it and see a text.

SmittenKitten: Thinking about you and that wonderful thing you do with your tongue. See you tonight at love shack?
ME: Absolutely
Me: Off duty @ 630 tonight - can be there by 635

SmittenKitten: I'll have dinner for us. Enjoy the rest of your day hot stuff.

Whistling I put my phone back in my pocket.

"Big smile on your face with a text message must be the reason for your good mood Sheriff. Glad to see something has you this happy again. I don't think I've seen a young lady on your arm since you retired from your service days."

"Gertie don't go snooping. Just something new and yes, it has put me in a good mood, and I'm going to enjoy it."

"You deserve to enjoy it, Garrett. You deserve all the happiness you find. You put your time in and we appreciate you around here more than you could ever measure but I like seeing that smile on your face. Whoever she is, I hope she treats you like you deserve to be treated. Here's your sandwich and potato salad. It's on me today. Your happy mood is rubbing off on me."

"Thank you, Gertie. I appreciate that very much! I'd better get back to the station. Have a good rest of your day!"

"You to Sheriff and enjoy your lady friend."

***

At my desk going through paperwork as usual, "Sheriff, you have a delivery," Katy my dispatcher says. "Here," she hands me a bag, "someone just dropped it off for you."

"Thanks."

After she leaves my office, I open the little bag and see a white Chinese take-out box. What in the world is this? I open it up and see a bunch of fortune cookies and a note.

Candles aren't the only thing getting blown tonight. Made these special for you. Remember to add....in bed, after your fortune.
Xoxo Smitten Kitten

Laughing I open the first cookie and the fortune reads, *before you receive, you must give.* Oh, this is fun, let's see what else she's got in mind, so I break open another cookie *You are talented with your hands.* One more just because these are damn tasty, and the fortune reads *You will soon get unexpected kisses in unexpected places.* I grabbed my phone to send Hill a text.

Me: thank you for my delicious fortune cookies and handwritten fortunes.
SmittenKitten: You are welcome. See you later *winking emoji*

My phone buzzes again. Thinking it must be Hill again I smile, only to see the text is from Rob and the guys.

Rob: I see you must have ditched us last night to go out for a date.
Me: What?
Jackson: I'm with Rob. Seeing someone new that we don't know about???
Noah: OOHH *curious emoji*
Coop: Wait what! What's going on?
Rob: Look at Gertie's Fb Page Harmony Hears
Rob: Seems our Sheriff couldn't stop smiling or WHISTLING!
Rob: Fucking Awesome. Deets NOW
Me: Nah, just something new-nothing big to share
Jackson: Right.
Coop: K
Jackson: You really are moving on from Hill huh? Whatever happened and then the cabin was enough to push you in a new direction
Me: New direction-yes
Noah: Happy for you man. Endings always suck but focus on the new
Me: Exactly

Fuck…damn it, Gertie. Your gossipy ears and eyes are too much.

HAPPY TOWN - HAPPY SHERIFF

Everyone be on your best behavior because our hard-working Sheriff Stone is in a good mood today and he deserves to stay that way. Keep up the good work Sheriff and keep whistling your happy tune.

My phone buzzes again.

Smitten Kitten: Careful now Hanky-pooh, Gertie has her radar on. What were you whistling? Kings Of Leon – Sex On Fire? *winking emoji*

I'll give her sex on fire later. Now, to stir up a little chaos among the gang. Tomorrow is Tuesday so the expectations are trivia night at Coopers Corner. So, let's get this Solo Pact going. Grabbing my phone, I start a group text.

**Me: Tomorrow Trivia Night @ Coops
Julia: yes, Jackson and I are coming
Ellen: Scott and me too
Stella: working co-DJ w Griff-C U there
Sam: Paul and I have a workshop-we are out-bummer
Bree: OH wings!!! The baby wants wings and curly fries!!!
Coop: Gotcha Bree *thumbs up emoji*
Bree: and Root beer. Lots of root beer with an orange slice
Rob: Gross
Noah: Be nice to my wife
Rob: Sorry Bree- orange+rootbeer =gross
Bree: I'll let you try it
Rob: hard pass- but thanks
Julia: Hill? Garrett? Um...
Smitten Kitten: I'm available
Me: I'm available**

Julia: ??
Julia: so, then….do we have to pick or will one of you say no???
Smitten Kitten: I'd really like to come
Me: Me too-you had them for pizza night though Hillary
Smitten Kitten: True.
Smitten Kitten: Ok, Garrett you can go to trivia night at Coops
Me: Are you sure?
Smitten Kitten: Yeah, it's your turn
Smitten Kitten: See-easy peasy
Rob: WTF was that?
Bree: Oh Fiddlesticks
Julia: Ohhkay…Hilly see you Thursday @ bookclub
Smitten Kitten: Perfect
Me: Guess you get me then. C U for trivia *smiley emoji*
Coop: Jesus

Chapter Twenty-Five

Garrett

I'm heading in to see Jackson for my yearly physical for the department today. It's nice that I know him and can use him as my doctor even though when it comes to certain appointments I don't go to my brother-in-law. For my standard physical for the department, it's nothing uncomfortable for either of us. I'm already in the exam room waiting for him.

The door opens and he walks in, "Hey man, good to see you. Seems like we just did your exam for the department. Where the heck has the last year gone?"

"No clue, I think we've all just been so busy with everything going on. First you and Jules and getting you through your issues and then Bree and fighting to keep her job, wedding, and baby. A lot has happened among all of us to keep us busy."

"Yeah, when you spell it all out like that it sure sounds like a lot. So how are you doing? I know things didn't end the way you had hoped with Hill and I'm sorry man, but maybe now that you guys talked you can figure out how to deal with everything and eventually it will go back to more normal. Between you and me, your sister is feeling bad that she forced both of you to deal with things and that they didn't end up in a pretty little package with a bow."

"Jackson, Jules shouldn't feel bad. The best part was that I finally got Hill to sit down and listen to me. I told her exactly how I felt, and we talked about what went down to put us in the situation we were in. Now we decided to take the time that we both need and just let the dust settle for a bit. Julia shouldn't feel bad about anything. I'm glad we ended up stuck at the cabin. Hillary was forced to finally stop and listen to me, otherwise, we'd still just be fighting in secret and I gotta tell ya, that wasn't working for me. I think we are finally at a good point where we can move on."

"But you're in love with her. How are you moving on with someone new when you can't have her? How are you managing that so quickly?"

"I just had to realize that I have to go for whatever it is that will make me happy, and I can't wait around for it to land in my lap. If I see something I go after it. I'm not happy that Hill and I lost so much time this year arguing and fighting but I am happy where we landed. It will be okay. Tell my sister not to worry so much. I'm good. I think Hillary is going to be fine too. You know there isn't much that keeps her down for long."

"That's true. As much as I hate this stupid solo pact thing you have going on now where we won't have both of you at the same time, I suppose it's fair to accept while you both figure things out personally."

"That's right."

"So, want to tell me why Gertie posted about you being all happy and whistling?"

"Nope."

"Not going to share anything?"

"Nope. Just something new I am enjoying at the moment."

"Well, we haven't seen you date so excuse us for noticing that you do seem happier than you've been."

"Jackson, I can't date around here. You know that, but I haven't been a monk either. There is a very good reason I don't date where I live, and you know that. Can you imagine if you weren't married, and you had to date? How well do you think that would work out for you? Everyone in town would know your business before they needed to. So, I date ladies that live a town or two away and stay out of Lake Harmony. Especially with gossip queens like Gertie. You should have seen her asking me questions the other day when I went in to order my lunch."

"Well, you gave her enough to warrant a FB post about your happiness and whistling," he says to me while laughing.

"Fuck you, man. She catches everything around here. You know how that works."

"Oh yeah, I try not to even go near her because she will read into any situation. Better you than me though."

***

Walking back to the station I see Carter, a regular townie, waving me down and heading over toward me, "Hey Sheriff, I saw some kids down at the park messing around. I don't like to rat them out because I was a teenager once too, but looked like they were smokin' some weed and starting to get a little rowdy. I just want to make sure they don't do something they are going to regret."

"Thanks, Carter, where exactly did you see them? I'll call it into one of my guys that are out patrolling."

"They are down at the little tot lot playground under the slides. Probably figured no little ones will be out playing in this cold weather."

"Well thanks again, I'll make sure to get someone over there right away. Speaking of the cold, where's your coat man? It can't be more than 50 degrees out here."

"Aw, I'm fine. The cold doesn't hurt me. See ya later Sheriff."

I watched him walk away and headed into the station.

"Katy, can you get one of the guys out to the tot lot at the park? Carter saw some kids that looked like they were smoking some pot. I don't want to do more than scare them, take their stash away and take them home to their parents. Have them head that way and if they need backup let me know. Not sure how many kids Carter saw."

"On it Sheriff."

Damn, teenagers. I don't know why they always head to the playgrounds. They pick the strangest spots around town to get into mischief. Another one of those, Carter was in the right place at the right time moments.

Chapter Twenty-Six

Hillary

I'm barely awake but I have food to prep for some events this weekend and I have book club with the girls. I was at the love shack again last night with Garrett and if we keep going at it like this, we are both going to die of sexual exhaustion. If that isn't a real thing yet, it will be.

"Knock, knock Hilly. Your coffee is here," Griff says as he brings in a coffee with a bag from Ellen's shop Harmonious Bites across the town square.

"Um… thanks, Griff. I need about ten more cups, but this is a great start."

"Yeah girl, you are looking like what the dirty cat dragged in after it smoked cracked with a hooker in the alley."

"Great. Get out, Griff. Too early."

He laughs, "No problem baby doll. I will come to check on you after the first coffee kicks in."

I looked into the bag and see my favorite orange scone. Thank you, baby Jesus for bringing me sustenance.

Me: <picture of coffee and scone> Is this your kindness and generosity keeping me alive this morning?

Hank-ServiceMan: Yes baby, I'm sorry I didn't let you sleep much last night but you were too hard to resist

Me: Back at you handsome- how did you manage this secretly

Hank-ServiceMan: I can't share all my secrets but there is this great thing called food delivery apps

Me: Smartass

Hank-ServiceMan: behave or your ass will get spanked later

Me: Promise?

Hank-ServiceMan: grrr I wish we were still in bed

Me: Me too but a girl has to sleep sometime *wink emoji*

Hank-ServiceMan: have fun w the girls tonight-keep your phone on you
Me: Have fun @ poker

I left work at 3 and went home to take a nap. Thank the heavens above that I get to be my own boss. Griffin finally kicked me out after nearly cutting my fingers off prepping food in the back. I slept for three hours so I'm heading over to Bree for book club.

I'm the last one here, so I rush to the front door and knock, but walk in, "Hello ladies…sorry I'm late." I headed back to the voices and find Julia, Bree, Sam, and Ellen all in the kitchen putting out the food they brought to share. I plunk down a plate of brownies I whipped up earlier. "Here, it's all I had time for today, so I am sorry but since Bree counts as two votes and loves chocolate I figured I'm safe with dessert."

"YESSSS," Bree says. "This baby loves spicy or sweet food. I don't know what the inside of my stomach is going to develop into by the time baby comes but for now, I'm just going with the flow."

"Great attitude," Julia says.

"Agree, you were so queasy in the first three months so if you are feeling better now, I say eat exactly what the cravings are telling you," Ellen says.

"True," Sam says. "If you nurse after the baby is born you won't be eating all that spicy food because you will have to be more careful not to eat something that will upset the baby's tummy."

"Oh my god, I am so excited for another little one to spoil rotten. How are the rest of you doing? We haven't had girl time since you abandoned me with Garrett at the cabin so spill," I say.

"Oh no, the one talking first is going to be you Hill," Julia says to me. "I am so sorry if doing that made things worse. The last thing I wanted was to push so hard that it made things worse for both of you. Are you upset with me?"

"No. I was. I mean you know how angry I was. There was a very good reason I was so angry. I don't want to talk about it but what I will say is that I trusted Garrett with anything you know, and then something happened, and he broke that trust. It wasn't something little, but it was a direct hit to my heart, and I never would have imagined that something like that would ever happen because of him. He was always the one there ready to pounce if we needed him and yet, he was the one that hurt me."

Bree puts her arms around me, "Are you sure you are okay now, or at least better? Things still seem shaky between you and Garrett."

"We talked, and I mean it this time. We each took turns talking about what happened and how we felt. Honestly, there was a huge break of communication which made it worse but when talking we realized how our actions had hurt each other. So, this solo pact, it's not nonsense. It is time for him and me to not be together with all of you in a situation where it will trigger any of those same emotions. We both just want some time to heal and get past it. You know we fought, made up but it's not like we can be besties yet. I hope that you understand and give us both time we asked for—okay?"

Julia hugs me, "As long as you are both okay, we can support you both and give you what you need although this solo pact thing feels weird."

"Yeah, it does," Sam says, "but I get it."

"We will do whatever you need and just be more cognizant of when we plan group things. We can also try to not make either of you feel left out," Ellen says.

"Anyway, enough talk of that. Let's talk about something else."

Bree smiles, "I have something else I want to ask all of you, I need to go register for the baby and pick out the baby's furniture. Would any of you like to come with me this weekend? Julia, I know you may be busy but I have no idea what I even need and hoped you could help. I've been looking online at other mommy-to-be sites and looking at their lists, but I'd like to pick your brain and get what's most needed. Then anything else that I get will be fun and extra."

"Of course, I can help Bree. Nothing would keep me from helping you with the baby. Do you have an idea of where you want to go," Julia asks.

"I thought just one of the big chain stores for the regular items for the registry and then I'm meeting mom and Noah's sister Shannon at a baby store for the furniture and stroller in the city. Whoever wants to go do both with me, lunch is on Noah. He wanted me to say that. I think he knows I will wear myself out otherwise and he wants you girls to keep an eye on me. Who's free Saturday?"

"I'm good during the day. I have an event that evening I can't miss," I say. I'm planning on spending the night and all day with Garrett, but they don't need to know that. Ellen and Sam are both free too so looks like we are all going.

"Since we are all going Bree, how about I drive us because I have the biggest vehicle? Just in case we end up needing the trunk space," Julia says.

"That's perfect. Mom will have her car too so we can always put the small bags in her car. If we end up buying some bigger things, they will fit in your car. Noah said to have the furniture delivered, if possible, if not can we borrow your van Hilly?"

"Absolutely, but they should be able to deliver and maybe even put the furniture together."

"Oh no, Noah won't let anyone put the crib together. He said he has dreamt all his life that he would get to put a crib together for his baby. For some reason, he thinks this is something he must do. Some misguided right of parenthood. I'll let you know how long it takes him because from what I've seen it's not a simple project," Bree says.

"I'll have Jackson on standby. That won't help much. For this I think Rob or Dad would be your best options," Julia says. "They are the builders in the family. Jackson has trouble with Legos."

Laughing, we all head into the family room with food and drinks. "So, did anyone read this book or are we just talking about life and enjoying each other's company?"

Chapter Twenty-Seven

Garrett

Poker night with the guys is always one of my favorite nights and this month we have a table full. My brother Rob is here, Noah and Jackson, Scott, Paul, and even Cooper.

"Who's ready to just hand me their money," Rob says.

"Wow, starting strong tonight already huh bro?"

"Well, Mr. Whistler because I have a new lady friend, I'm sure your head won't be in the game. Noah is thinking about his baby on the way, Scott and Paul just don't play a good game of poker, Jackson is on call tonight and not paying attention, and Coop…he'd be my only true competitor tonight."

"Always a pleasure to take your money Rob," Cooper says.

"Don't be a dick, the guys may all have other things on their minds, but they need an estrogen break too. So be cool or I'll just take your money and throw you out."

"Fine, but don't say I didn't warn you," Rob says.

Jackson laughs, "I'm with Rob though, anything new you want to share regarding your whistling or the reason for it?"

"Nope." Giving the guys all my shitty big grin, "I'm not sharing anything."

"I'm curious as to how you met someone so quickly since you've been pining after Hillary forever and I didn't know you'd been dating much this year," Cooper asks.

"Someone I've known that just came back around is all."

"Uh huh, and you're this smitten already," Cooper asks again. "Fine, I know you will tell me when you're ready."

I look over at my best friend, who knows me, and my secrets and knows there is something I'm hiding. I just give him our nod and he knows to trust me here. There's more to the story but now isn't the time. He nods back.

"Well, let's get this game started," Cooper says. "I don't know about all of you but I'm ready to take all of Rob's hard-earned cash away from him tonight."

"Sounds good to me," I say.

Cooper wins the first game, and we stop and grab pizza and beer before we continue. Jackson has barely taken two bites of pizza and his phone goes off. "Crap, it's the on-call service. Let me see what's up." He gets up and walks into the other room to talk on the phone.

"So, what's new with any of you guys? Anything exciting happening lately?"

Noah laughs, "Yeah, so when Bree and I went to LA and I hung out with Jax Turner and the Brick Row rock band I got to know them pretty well. One of the guys from the band, Mattie the drummer, is married and has kids. He got my number while I was there so he would have a doctor he trusted to talk to and not someone who would just tell him whatever because of who he is. Anyway, he face-timed me with his wife over the weekend because all his kids ended up with chicken pox. He didn't believe his wife that the kids had chicken pox because they were vaccinated but they did. He even held one of the kids up to the camera so I could see it. I tried explaining to him that even with the vaccine the kids could still get it just usually not as severe a case. Then the next day he called me back because he had chicken pox. I guess his mom thought he'd had them as a kid but couldn't remember. Anyway, for an adult, it's serious so I told him to call his doctor and see if he'd give him some anti-viral drugs to avoid more complications."

"I can't imagine getting them as an adult. I remember one of us came down with chicken pox and Mom put all of us together in the same room, so we'd all get them and be done with them. I think even the girls, Sam and Bree, came over because I remember it was like summer break, but we should have been in school. We just played and all the moms helped us with our schoolwork."

Noah says, "That was very smart to get it over with when you were all little. Now the vaccine helps, but nothing is foolproof."

"It's still so weird that you are buddies with Brick Row. I love that band," Rob says.

"Yeah, they're so cool and normal. Mattie said they are going on tour next year and if they come through Chicago to let him know how many tickets we want."

"Oh my god, that's awesome! I'm in," Rob says.

Jackson comes back into the room and sits down, "All good. Just had to make a call and check on an expecting mom who was nervous. What's up."

Noah smiles, "I was just about to ask all of you who may be interested in helping me paint the nursery as a surprise for Bree Saturday. She can't be around the fumes and her mom and Shannon are taking her out baby shopping and doing the baby registry. She's asking them tonight at their book club. I could use a few helpers so I can paint the nursery and have it done in a day. Any takers?"

"I'd be happy to help. Count me in," I say.

"Me too. I don't have anything going on this weekend," Rob adds.

"I have staff out this weekend, so I have to cover the restaurant and bar, but if you need more help another time, just ask," Cooper adds.

"I'm in," Scott says.

"I have a couple of new Veterans coming in this weekend to start at the nursery, so I won't be able to help you out. Sorry Noah," Paul says.

"I think we should have enough hands-on deck with Garrett, Rob, Jackson, and Scott. I want to repaint the ceiling and then we are doing a soft blue tone on the walls."

"Wait, are you having a boy," Rob asks.

Noah answers, "Don't know yet, but Bree and I are doing a nautical theme, so she picked blue for the walls like water. She said it is a calming color."

"True, I don't think colors mean as much these days anymore either. Colors are binary now," Rob says.

"Look at you little brother with the big words," I tease.

"Hey, I am just aware of what is happening around me. I want to be an equal employer and non-judgmental. That's all."

"Nah, just teasing. I agree Rob. Things like that just don't matter anymore and a little girl can be captain of her ship just as much as a little boy."

"True, so painting, and then she doesn't know it but I already bought the crib and the rocker she put on her list. So, if it's okay with you I want to attempt to put the crib together while we get the room painted so that when she comes home, she has the crib and rocker already in the room," Noah says.

"Bree is going to be so happy," Jackson says. "What else do you need for the baby's room?"

"I was going to ask Rob if he could build something for me," Noah asks.

"Sure buddy, whatcha need?"

"I want to have one of those bookshelves that looks like a boat or canoe tipped on its end. Do you know what I'm talking about?"

"Yeah, if you want Dad still has some of our old canoes in the shed. Bree may get a kick out of me using one of those and turning it into a bookshelf. What do you think about that? I mean she probably used it as much as Garrett and I have. She was always around when we were growing up."

"I like that idea and it brings some of her childhood into the baby's room. Perfect. I will let you decide how it looks. I don't care if you keep it looking rustic, old, and used like it is or if you want to paint it."

"All our boats and canoes have names painted on them. That was something that Dad always made us do. Any time we got a new boat it needed a name," Rob says.

"Hey, do we still have that yellow canoe that the girls always claimed was theirs," I ask Rob. "Didn't they name it Sunny Days?"

"That's the boat I'm thinking about. I think so, it would be cute in here for a girl or boy. I will go by Mom and Dad tomorrow and look to see. If there are a few choices I can send you a text with a picture but that is the one, I think Bree would love."

Chapter Twenty-Eight

Hillary

Baby shopping with Bree turns into an emotional day for all of us. Bree continues to break down in tears of excitement and worry that she won't know what to do with a newborn. Thankfully, her mom and Julia have experience and are calming her down as she builds necessities on her registry.

Sitting down at the rockers Bree looks up as she wipes her tears away again, "I feel weird building this registry. Are people going to think I'm crazy for putting a breast pump on there?"

"No way, go ahead and add all the things you are going to need. People love buying gifts for babies and this is your first one, so most people will know that you are starting from scratch," Julia says. "I love buying things for babies and I don't have any so now I get to spoil yours. We will plan your shower a couple of months before the baby is due so that you have time to see what you still need to buy yourself. Honestly, I don't think you've registered for enough items. Let's go back through the infant things and add some more items. You also should add a second nursing pillow. That way you can have one upstairs and downstairs and not have to lug it back and forth. Let's also add some bottles and things you will use daily. It's easier to have more than enough of some items so you don't waste your time constantly cleaning out used bottles," Julia says.

"Okay, thanks, you guys. This is the rocker I registered for. It's so comfortable and pretty. I can't wait to be in the nursery rocking the baby," Bree says.

"Well, as beautiful as it is, let's keep you going because we need to get you to lunch so you don't fizzle out on us. The hard stuff is done, so let's finish this up," I say.

***

We are sitting at the restaurant finishing our lunch when my phone starts buzzing. I discreetly pulled my phone out of my pocket.

Hank-ServiceMan: Hey beautiful, thinking of you
Me: Aw, feeling lonely?
Hank-ServiceMan: Always- when I'm not with you. How's shopping?
Me: Done- now at lunch. You?
Hank-ServiceMan: Finishing up over here too
Hank-ServiceMan: Date Night- Dress up for me. I'm taking you on a sexy date later to show you off
Me: Hmm...that sounds romantic
Hank-ServiceMan: I hope so *winking emoji* meet@630 we have about a 40 min drive

I hear a clearing of throats and look up at everyone staring at me with goofy grins. *Busted.*

"Oh, you better start talking Hill because you are smiling big and happy right now. What's going on with you to make you smile like that," Julia asks.

"Work."

"I call bullshit," Shannon says. "That text must have been from a man. Are you dating someone, Hillary?"

"I thought you were on a man break," Bree asks.

"Just having a little bit of fun. I just got asked on a date."

"Whomever he is and can put that smile on your face sweetheart, maybe a keeper. Just have fun and don't fret," Bree's mom says.

"Absolutely, have fun and don't put pressure on yourself," Julia says, "Just go with the flow and see what happens."

"Hank huh," Sam asks. That's what your phone said, "Hank the serviceman."

"Yep, Hank...and his services are Ah-mazing," I add with a sexy laugh.

Chapter Twenty-Nine

Garrett

We are at Noah's helping him paint the room for the baby while the girls are keeping Bree busy. As I'm finishing the trim, I hear Noah and Rob in the other room laughing and swearing and go peek in.

"How is it possible that putting a crib together can be so fucking difficult! I've been working on this for hours," Noah says.

"Jesus, I think building a house is a faster process. What are all these different screws for? I hope they give you twenty extra just in case or you've not put that thing together the right way," Rob laughs.

"I followed the directions but this is a crib that also turns into a day bed so there are a ton of pieces that we don't need for the crib but need to keep for the next phase bed. I am starting to think once we have the crib together it's a done deal. I'd rather go buy a new bed frame when the baby outgrows this thing. I'm exhausted," Noah says.

"At this point, I agree with you," Rob says. "Let's get this thing finished up so we can drag it into the baby's room. You did make sure it will fit through the doorway, right?"

"Fuck, no. That would have been a better plan, huh? Can we take that one side back off so we can angle it in there? Help me hold this for a second Rob."

Leaning against the door frame, "Hey, need some help in here," I ask.

"Yeah, let's get this in the nursery before we finish putting it together, and before you hit the trim around the door," Noah adds.

We managed to get the crib and rocker into the nursery and clean up the tarps on the floor from painting.

"Wow!" Noah says while looking at the room and his baby's crib and rocker. "This doesn't seem real. I can't believe I'm going to be a dad soon."

I grip his shoulder, "You are going to be an awesome dad, Noah. I'm so happy for you and Bree. This baby is going to be one loved kiddo."

Rob stands there pushing against the crib, "This seems sturdy, so I think it's safe to put your kid in here. I am going to head out and grab the bookcase. Are one of you going to be here to help carry it in? I already cut the canoe in half and added a new base to it this morning, then sealed it with a clear shellack so it should be dry. Let's see if we can get that in here too before Bree gets home."

"If it's okay with Noah, I'm going to head out. I have a date tonight," I say.

"Go ahead Garrett," Noah says. "I appreciate all your help guys especially since Scott couldn't come help. I know you have better things to do on your day off than paint a nursery."

"Nah man, I'd do anything for Bree. She's like another sister to me," Rob says. "I'll go check the bookshelf and be right back Noah."

"I'll head out with you Rob, and you know we are always happy to help. That's what friends do man."

My phone buzzes in my pocket and I pull it out and see a text from Hillary.

SmittenKitten: Hey sexyman. Heading home for date. Decided not to wear anything sexy underneath.
Me: Why not *Sad emoji*
SmittenKitten: Not wearing ANYTHING
Me: I may not make it through dinner
SmittenKitten: You promised me a date night- Don't make me put granny panties on to punish you
Me: You could make granny panties sexy baby
SmittenKitten: Is that right? LOL
Me: Absolutely

"What's this Smitten Kitten big brother," Rob asks leaning over me and looking at my phone.

"The woman I have been seeing."

"Good for you Garrett, I am glad you are dating someone. Smitten Kitten…who's that," Noah asks.

"Nothing either of you need to know. See you both later." I say and leave with a smile on my face.

***

I've dressed in my black slacks and blue dress shirt and a little bit nervous pacing around the rental house and waiting for Hillary to get here so we can leave for our date. I heard the garage door go up and a few moments later see her come into the house.

Her brown hair is curled and bouncing softly around her face. She doesn't usually wear too much makeup, but she has her eyes smoky and soft pink on her lips. She looks up and sees me staring at her and smiles.

"Wow, don't you look handsome G. I love that blue on you. It makes your eyes pop," she says.

"You look beautiful Hill, are you ready to head out?"

"I am. Where are we going tonight?"

"There's a new restaurant that opened in Geneva, Illinois that is supposed to be good. I thought we could head out there and enjoy ourselves."

"Sounds perfect. What kind of food do they have?"

"It's a steak house and overlooks the river. I reserved a table with a view. Before we head out though I need to do something first."

"Okay, I'm ready whenever you are ready to go."

I walk over to her and put my hand on the back of her neck and pull her into me for a kiss. I kiss the edge of her lip and then slide my mouth over hers. Her arms come around me and she deepens the kiss. After a few moments I pulled away and put my head against hers, "You are beautiful but I couldn't leave without kissing you first. You ready to go now?"

"If you don't drag me out of here immediately, I'm going to tear your clothes off your body and have my way

157

with you. Steak sounds good though, so let's go before I change my mind."

I give her one more quick kiss and pull her out towards the garage, "Let's go so I can get back and have my dessert."

Chapter Thirty

Garrett

It's Tuesday and I'm sure the texts are going to start up about trivia night at Coopers Corner. I'm finishing up the schedule for the next month when Jilly, my receptionist pokes her head into my office.

"Sheriff, you have a delivery. The note says it's from your smitten kitten."

"How do you know what the note says Jilly," I ask.

"Because I opened it to see who the delivery was for. Who's a smitten kitten? Are you dating a stripper? I won't tell anyone because that is your business but if that's the kind of lady you date you should probably not bring her around here with that name," she adds.

"Jilly, can I have the delivery, please? No, she is not a stripper that is only her nickname."

"Oh, thank God, because Sherriff that would be a bit awkward now wouldn't it."

"Jilly, the delivery?"

"Oh, yes, here it is." She hands me a small box and leaves my office.

Hillary, you are getting brave in your delivery game. I open the box and see a coin. It has two different sides to it. One side reads *Flip to decide what it will be-- His Choice* and the other side reads *Flip to decide what it will be-- Her Choice*. There's a small note written and laid inside with the coin.

Hanky- thought this decision coin would be fun for whose turn it is to be in charge xoxo Smitten Kitten

Smiling I grab my phone and turn the coin, so *His Choice* is facing up and take a picture. Then send her a text.

Me: Flipped and this was face up *picture of coin*
Me: Looks like I'm in charge tonight.
SmittenKitten: yummy
SmittenKitten: Time to stir the pot-trivia
Me: Okay LOL

I get up to go grab another cold drink from the staff area and come back to see a group text coming through that Hillary has started.

SmittenKitten: Hey gang, who's going to trivia tonight?
Julia: Jackson and I-with kids
Rob: Me
Ellen: Scott and I are out-sorry guys
Griffin: Stella and I will be there hosting
Sam: Paul and I are thinking about it
Bree: YES!!!! Wings and Fries!!!!
Rob: No root beer with oranges Bree?
Noah: That a real question Rob?
Rob: Yep
Bree: Yes root beer too w fruit-cherries this time
Rob: Ugh gross again but better than oranges
SmittenKitten: I am out. I am exhausted and have a big week with holiday lunches. Let Garrett go this time.

I send a quick text to add my input…

Me: Oh, I have to work. You go Hill. It's okay. I think it's my turn but you can take it and then I can switch with you and take the next one.
SmittenKitten: No, really Garrett, I am sooo tired. I am not going out tonight.
Me: Are you sure?
SmittenKitten: Well, maybe I could go for dinner, so I don't have to cook

They are hating us right now. Laughing I add another text to the group.

Me: Okay see.
Julia: See you tonight then *Smiling emoji*
SmittenKitten: No, I better stay home and rest. Thanks though
Coop: Jesus you two. I'm exhausted now
Julia: We will miss both of you. ALSO-this Saturday is Friends White Elephant Christmas at our house and you BOTH better be there at the same time. No exceptions/excuses. This is a holiday and you both need to suck it up and deal for a few hours.
Me: Okay Jules. No worries-Hillary and I will make an exception
SmittenKitten: It is a holiday so I suppose we can cooperate a little

Laughing at the reactions of my friends I sent Hill a quick text.

Me: You really staying home tonight?
SmittenKitten: Hell no, the coin says it's your choice tonight and I want to see what your choice is. I will be ready and waiting for you @ love shack

***

We are lying in bed about to fall asleep when Hill puts her chin on my chest and looks up at me. I touch her face and run my thumb over her cheekbone. "You okay baby?"

"Yes, sometimes I just stop and pinch myself. Do you ever think about us, about this?"

"I always think about you Hill, what's the matter?"

"Sometimes I still can't believe we are where we are. Two weeks ago, I was ready to kill you. I was so mad and now I can't stand being away from you. It's just strange. Sometimes it feels like it isn't real and then sometimes it feels like it's always been this way between us. I know it's new, but G I honestly can't imagine my life without you in it this way. That scares me. Does it scare you?"

"Babe, I'm not scared anymore because this is exactly where I want to be. I am so happy that you are here snuggled in my arms, naked, and that you are mine." I kiss her and roll her under me. "Now, stop worrying, and let me show you how happy I am that you are here with me and that I am never letting you get away again. I think the coin toss means it's my decision for the entire night."

"Oh, and what is it you want to do? You've already ravished me tonight."

"It's still early and I haven't had my fill of you yet. So, how about I start kissing you all over and you tell me if I am hot or cold."

"This is fun, right now your mouth needs to be on me looking for the hot zones. Ready, set, go!"

I nip her jawline and go to her neck just below her ear when I hear her say, "Warmer."

I smile and keep moving down her body licking and sucking her breasts, "Warmer," she says again.

"Mmm, I better keep going so I don't fall into the cold zone."

"Right now, you are talking and very very cold," she says.

I move back to her breast and run my tongue around her nipple, "I hope I am getting warmer."

"Oh yes, very warm," she says.

I kiss down her belly and run my tongue around her belly button and hear her moan, moving across to her hip and nipping and then kissing it, then move back with my tongue across to her belly button, dip a lick lower but not where I know she needs me to be. I move back up and hear, "Colder." Yeah baby, I know, but I'll get there soon. I kiss and nip her other hip then move back to her belly button and lick lower again. I feel her trying to push me where she needs me but it's not going to be that easy. I move down and instead of hitting her center where she wants me, I move to her inner thigh and down to her inner knee.

"Much much colder down there G," she says a bit frustrated.

I lift my head, "Oh? Is there something you need baby?"

"Please lick my pussy G. I need your mouth to stop the talking and start the licking. Make me come before I scream."

"I will make you scream baby just be patient, I still have to taste your other thigh."

I hear her let out a frustrated sigh so I move from one leg across to the other and pause to blow warm air on her center. She lifts towards my mouth, so I give a slow lick across her clit and hear her moan. Before I can get to lost in that I move to her other thigh and hear her again.

"Jesus, you are killing me. Please just make me come and stop dicking around down there."

"Okay baby, I've got you. I wanted to edge you out a little bit but I'll give you what you need." I close my mouth over her and lick and suck because I know she is close. She grabs my head and holds me there afraid I won't give her what she craves. I add a finger and curl it to hit that special spot and suck her clit into my mouth. Her back rises off the bed and her feet wrap around me. I feel her body start to orgasm and hear her moan as I continue to lick her through all the spasms. I can't get enough of her taste. She is so sweet, and she is all mine.

I move back up her body and kiss her. "Feel better now Hill?"

"Yes, but I need a little more. Let's see if you can make it a twofer. Not sure you have it in you though."

"A twofer baby? I've already given you three orgasms since dinner. Let's go for a quadruple."

"No more talking, show me what you've got big guy."

Chapter Thirty-One

Hillary

This morning when I woke up in bed, I had time to look at Garrett while he was still asleep. He is such a good-looking man with his dark hair and his thick dark lashes. I never thought this would be the man that could steal my heart, but he has. I've always loved him, and he always had a special place in my heart but I didn't expect him to be someone I'd fall in love with and have as a partner. He makes me feel safe and loved, he makes me feel like he needs me to breathe. I've never felt this kind of connection with another person. It scares me but it also puts those damn butterflies in my belly. Knowing he feels the same way about me makes me nervous. What does that mean? Where do we go from here? Are we crazy to have fallen so hard in just a few weeks?

I'm at the office going through billing and paperwork for upcoming holiday parties when Griffin walks into my office.

"Hilly, you have a delivery."

"Bring it over here."

"I don't know who Hank is, but he knows you well, doesn't he?"

"Why? Why do you say that?"

Laughing and throwing his hand at me as he walks back out of my office, "Just read the note doll. All I'm saying."

I grab the note off the delivery box and open the card and smile. I peek into the box and see a variety of succulents.

Baby, I thought about sending you flowers but when I went to the florist, I saw these. They told me they are succulents. They reminded me of you…prickly but beautiful. Love, Hank

Me: prickly huh? You were saved with ...and beautiful

Hank-ServiceMan: Gotta keep you on your toes so you don't get bored with me

Me: I see. If I'm prickly then you are a mosquito bite I like to continue to scratch

Hank-ServiceMan: Oh I can keep biting if that makes you happy

Me: Yes, please

Me: I need to go to the city tonight for some supplies. Want to join me?

Hank-ServiceMan: Only if I can take you to dinner while we are out.

Me: Done, and G thank you for thinking of me.

Hank-ServiceMan: I'm always thinking of you, baby

I run through the last of my billing and go look for Griffin. I want to see if he can handle something for me later. We just got a last-minute holiday dinner catering request and I have to hit the city but maybe if he's free he can handle the request.

"Griff, any chance you want to handle a holiday dinner request that came in earlier? It's a small party over at the village hall for about a dozen people. I already have a run into the city scheduled to pick up supplies. It's a small group and there's just set up and clean up needed. You could take one staff member to help if you need to. I know a couple of them are looking for more hours for bulking up their savings."

"I can do that. I don't have anything else going on tonight. Do you need me to help prep the food or do we have enough here to handle their request?"

"If you want to help me, it will go faster. They just want some chicken breasts, potatoes, and salad. I thought we'd either give them brownies or cobbler for dessert."

"Oh Hilly, let me whip up my blueberry cobbler. You know Roxy can never get enough of it."

"Okay, go right ahead. Their dinner should be set up at five and then dinner served by six. If you want to call one of the team staff in, you can. Just let me know so I add those hours to their week.”

***

Garrett and I are heading back from the city with my supplies. Since there shouldn’t be anyone around, he is helping me unload the supplies in the shop.

I feel arms come around me from behind, “Mm, watching you keep bending over to put those supplies away has me needing to touch you,” he says.

“Oh yeah? Does my ass in these jeans turn you on,” I ask.

“Baby, everything about you turns me on. Have you ever fooled around in your shop?”

“No, I have a no-sex rule in my kitchen. I can’t prepare food where sex happens.”

“That’s not what you said at the house.”

“I don’t prepare food for paying customers at the love shack G. Here I need to be more careful.”

“How about your office? Do you prepare food in there or can we fool around on your desk?”

I grabbed his hand and drag him back to my office and shut the door. “Take off your pants G.”

“Oh? Did you get the coin toss and it says that it was your choice today,” he asks.

“If you don’t want a blow job tonight that’s fine. If you do though, strip.”

He moves his hands to his jeans and slowly unbuttons the top and starts moving his hips.

Smiling and holding back a chuckle I ask, “Are you giving me a strip tease Hank?”

“Is it turning you on?”

“It will if you start moving your hips and maybe lose the shirt. I’d like to watch some of my own private Magic Mike if you want to deliver.”

167

His eyes sparkle and he gives me a sexy grin. I watch as he takes his hand behind his head and pulls his Henley over his head. He's standing there with no shirt, and jeans unbuttoned and moves to his zipper all while moving his hips and shoulders in a sexy dance.

"I could get used to this," I say as I move towards him and run my hands over his chest and start to move down towards his sculpted abs. "How do you keep yourself so chiseled? It's totally not fair but please keep it up because I'm going to follow your abs with my tongue."

"Hill, if you do that I may not get through this dance."

"Oh, don't worry G, I promise you will end with a happy ending tonight."

I lick my way down and help him with the jeans that are now loosely hanging on his hips. I pull jeans and boxers down and his erection is mine for the taking. I slowly lick from base to tip and run my tongue around the crown of his erection.

I hear him suck in a breath and moan, "So fucking good."

I slowly run my tongue down the side of him and gently grab his balls with my other hand. I know what my man likes and now I must decide if I give him what he needs or tease him a bit as he does to me. I moved my mouth back to his crown and put my mouth around him. His breathing is labored and he's holding my head in his hands. I can take him deep and I know he's waiting for it, but he doesn't push me. He lets me be in charge, for now.

I continue to move my mouth up and down him and I know he's close. I put pressure on his balls and his breathing changes.

"Hill, I'm going to come."

I continue to suck him harder and after a few more sucks he begins to come in my mouth, and I swallow everything he gives me. He puts his hands under my arms and pulls me to stand.

"Fuck, your mouth is fucking amazing. I need to pay you back." His hands moved to my pants but I put my hand over his.

"I need you in me, but I want a bed, not my desk. Can you put a pause on my turn until I get you back to the love shack?"

"Are we done here?"

"Yep, just need to lock up and get there."

"Let's go!"

We step out of my office and turn the corner to head to the back door and see Griff standing in the kitchen with a red face.

"Um, hey you two," he says with embarrassment. "Was hoping to be out of here before you came out of the office."

Griff is looking back and forth from me to Garrett, and we watch as the pieces click and he gets a smile on his face, "Ah, this must be Hanky baby, huh?"

"Griff," Garrett says.

"No worries love birds; I see what's going on here. No sexy times in the kitchen but the office is a free zone, or so I hear," he says with a wink. "I can keep a secret. I was just bringing some things back from the village. Don't mind me. I didn't know I was going to interrupt sexy times. Please continue."

"And we are leaving. Please keep this quiet Griff. Garrett and I are seeing where things go before, we want everyone to know."

"Aw Hilly bean, you know I just want you happy. If this big muscle man does it for you, then enjoy. Didn't see…or hear…anything." He waves and wanders out the door.

"Great. I know Griff is good with secrets, but I guess we hope it stays quiet a little longer."

"Babe, he won't say anything. Don't worry. We don't have to let the troops know until we are ready to. Let's go. I need to get you naked and under me soon."

Chapter Thirty-Two

Hillary

It's Christmas Eve and we are celebrating at Jackson and Julia's house with our traditional progressive dinner and white elephant gift exchange. The rules have changed over the years for gifts, we now give nice white elephant gifts instead of gag gifts but there is still a twenty-five dollar limit. The girls give to the girls and the guys give to the guys. Garrett and I both agreed to go so we are careful not to be too cozy around each other.

Our dinner is broken into categories and each of us is responsible for different parts: Drinks, appetizers, salad/bread, soup, main course, and dessert. Our drinks for the evening are courtesy of Garret, Rob, and Cooper and they brought a variety of Old Fashion, Gin & Tonic, Prosecco, or sparkling cider for Bree. Everyone has a drink in hand, and we are all hanging around the kitchen and family room enjoying the appetizer charcuterie board provided by Ellen and Scott.

Garrett and I keep circling opposite each other, not talking, trying not to continuously look at each other, but staying civil from a distance. Harder to do than we both expected.

"Let's move to the dining room and start with soup and salad everyone," Julia says.

"Let me help you bring food to the table, Jules," I say and move into the kitchen. Everyone else moves into the dining room while Julia ladles soup into the soup bowls and I start taking them into the dining room and placing them in front of each person. I look up and see that the empty place setting for me is directly opposite Garrett. Only three feet separating us tonight at the table but being able to look right into his eyes will be interesting.

Once we have the soup and salad at the table Julia and I go and join the others. Jackson raises his glass in a toast, "To all my favorite people sitting here around this table. It's been a bumpy year for us but together we can get through anything. To you, your friendship, and to next year bringing a healthy baby for Bree and Noah, and love and happiness to all of you. Cheers!"

We all clink our glasses against each other's, me avoiding Garrett until I can't. "Cheers, I say to him."

"To love and happiness Hill," he replies with a smile and clinks his glass against mine.

I quickly peek around the table at everyone else. Only Julia seems to have caught that toast between the two of us and she has a teary smile on her face. Griffin also caught it but instead of sappy, he looks like someone with a secret and a big smile. I just rolled my eyes and act as if it didn't just mean the world to me, that he snuck in that toast with me.

We move into our main course and then dessert. After everyone has finished their meal, we all help Julia and Jackson clean up the food and move into the family room where all of our white elephant gifts are laying under the tree.

The gifts from the guys all have a blue sticker and the gifts from the girls all have a red sticker. We've done this so often that we know how to take a color-coordinating gift and one that we haven't brought ourselves. Typically, Bree acts as Santa Claus and makes sure to deliver the gifts to each of us. This year, Noah is wearing the Santa hat.

"Sorry guys, but me getting up and down for this year's white elephant gifts is just too much with my baby belly so I voted Noah to replace me," Bree says. "Plus, he looks yummy wearing that Santa hat."

"I would do anything you tell me to honey," Noah says. "Now you tell me what I need to do."

"Jackson and Julia get to go first since they hosted. Jackson, which gift do you want?"

Jackson tells Noah which gift to grab for him and he opens it. It's a big box and inside he pulls a tabletop bonsai tree. "This is cool, let me guess it's from Paul?"

Julia selects her gift and opens a cool veggie spiralizer tool. "This is much easier than the one that I have. This thing is electric which means I just push a button. Who brought this?"

Sam says, "I did, and I just got the same one. I loved it so much that I figured I would gift it this year."

Scott goes next and opens a small barrel of Whiskey from Jackson. Ellen selects a Williams Sonoma apron from Hillary. Sam gets a bathtub caddy tray from Julia. Paul chooses solar lanterns from Scott. Cooper selects an iPhone armband for running. Garrett picks Carhartt suede work gloves from Rob. Noah picks his gift of a cool cocktail shaker set from Cooper. Bree gets bath salts and oils made by Stella. Griffin picks a utility pocket knife from Garrett. Stella's gift is hot chocolate and a cute Santa mug from Bree. I got a mix of different coffee beans from Ellen. Rob is last to pick and gets a t-shirt with a big picture of Griffin smiling on it.

"Oh my god! Griff this is amazing," Rob says. He whips his sweater off over his head and puts the t-shirt on. "Perfect fit. I will wear this all the time Griff."

I look over at Griffin and he is blushing. "It's just a silly gift, Rob. You don't have to wear it."

"What? Why wouldn't I want to wear it? Griff man, this is awesome. I think you should autograph it for me though. Jules, do you have a Sharpie?"

She smiles and jumps up to grab it. Jackson looks at the shirt and says, "Hey Griff, can I get one of those too?"

"Wha…what? Why? Do you really want one," Griff asks.

"I just thought it would be cool to wear on trivia night and support you since you help Coop out as the host of trivia."

"You guys, I know we don't do gag gifts, so this was just something silly. I didn't expect you to actually wear it," Griff says.

"Nonsense," Rob says. "I will wear it all the time. I think it's hilarious and it's going to be a great pickup chick's shirt. The women are going to want to know who you are, and it will be a great conversation starter. Thanks, man. I love it."

I get up and go to the kitchen and Julia follows me in. "Hey, do you need help with any other cleanup while I am here?"

"No, you all were a great help already. I think other than everyone's last glass I'm done, and they just go into the dishwasher."

"Okay, just don't want to leave you and Jackson with a mess for Christmas morning with the kids. Where are they tonight? Figured they would be here."

"They didn't want to hang with all of us old people, so they went out with Mom and Dad for dinner and are driving through that house that does the big light show every year."

"That sounds like a lot of fun. Was Santa good to them this year?"

"Neither will be disappointed. Although the older they get the more expensive they are since they both asked for technology and electronics. Hill, I appreciate that you and Garrett have been here tonight at the same time, and it was nice seeing you so civil to each other. Can I hope that things may be moving back to normal soon?"

"Jules, we aren't monsters. We can be in the same place without being jerks to each other."

"Maybe it helps that you both seem to have someone new in your lives making each of you happy?"

I smile at her, "It doesn't hurt that is for sure."

She gives me a big hug, "I'm so glad you have someone that is making you happy. You do seem calmer lately."

I whisper in her ear, "It's all the fabulous sex I'm getting."

"Good for you Hill, good for you. You deserve it." She winks and heads back to the family room. I look at Garrett and he casually winks at me.

I refill my drink and walk back into the room where everyone is discussing New Year's Eve and their plans. Bree and Noah are inviting whoever is free over to their house.

"Sorry, everyone but I have an event that night."

Griff quickly looks over at me. Damn, I forgot that we marked that off the calendar this year to have free. "Hill, do you need me to help with that event or are you covered," he adds with a smirk.

That shithead is going to make me sit here and lie even more. "I told you; I've got it covered. You can make plans to ring in the new year without worrying about the event."

"It's just such a bummer you have to work, especially since you have to stay overnight for clean up the next day."

I'm staring at him, and he just winks. Silly Griffin, did you just give me an out with everyone? Maybe him being in on our little secret isn't such a bad thing after all.

"Sorry guys, but I will probably be on duty. You know with the holiday and drinking a lot of people get back on the road when they shouldn't. I'll probably take the shift, so we have enough manpower," Garrett says.

Griffin looks at Garrett, "That's true. That probably takes you out the whole night too, doesn't it? Bummer but nice of you to take such good care of us."

"You guys have fun though. I'll toast you from my event," I say. "I'm going to head out. I hope all of you have a great Christmas with your families tomorrow. I'm heading to my parents for the day, so I better get going since it's an early drive out."

"Thank you for coming Hill, let me go grab your coat."

I get all wrapped up in my warm coat, hat, and mittens. The temps are dropping tonight, and I hate being cold. "Thanks again for hosting and you have a great Christmas morning with the kiddos."

"Merry Christmas Hill. I hope Santa brings you something good and hug your parents from me. Think of me when you are eating your moms' cheesy potatoes tomorrow."

I give her one last hug and head to the car. While it's warming up I send Garrett a text.

Me: hurry up studmuffin. I'm cold and need to be warmed up

I put the car in drive and headed over to the love shack to put on my silky red nightie and Santa hat. The first round of gift-giving is about to start.

Chapter Thirty-Three

Garrett

It's the Monday after Christmas and I'm on duty at the station while everyone else is out shopping the sales. Hillary and I spent Christmas Eve and Christmas morning in bed together. I can't stop thinking about walking into the house with her wearing that red sexy silk number and a Santa hat and all the sex that came after. I love that she is finally letting down her walls with me and letting me see the tender side of her. I've known it was there all these years, it was just heavily protected.

For Christmas, I gave her two nights away for New Year's in Galena, Illinois at the Goldmoor Inn, a romantic B&B that overlooks the Mississippi River. My buddy is friends with the executive chef that makes delicious food and they have secluded cabins that will deliver breakfast to your door. This will allow me to wine and dine her with the chef's seven-course New Year's Eve dinner without everyone finding out. I've been enjoying our little secret of learning to be a couple and not having to share details or get opinions from our friends, except for Griffin. We leave Friday after work and don't come back until Sunday.

Jilly knocks on my door and pokes her head in, "Delivery for you Sheriff."

"Did you read the card on this one too?"

"Nope. The envelope was sealed," she answers with a smirk and lays the gift on my desk, and walks out.

I open the box and pull out a shirt. It has a big heart on the front and reads *You are my favorite boyfriend*. I laugh and shake my head. I am so wearing this on our weekend getaway. She has no idea that she is getting a surprise delivery today too. I grab my phone and send off a text.

Me: Thank you for my awesome shirt. I promise to wear it all the time.
SmittenKitten: You better *winking emoji*

I get back to work while waiting to see when she gets her surprise. I sent her a candle that smells like vanilla spice- which is her favorite. The label reads *I love you for your personality, but your boobs are a huge bonus.*

SmittenKitten: Thank you Hanky-smells so good! <pic of candle burning>
SmittenKitten: Glad the girls make you so happy
Me: I do enjoy them. Very much
SmittenKitten: I enjoy it when you enjoy them
Me: I enjoy every inch of you and can't wait to have you again later
SmittenKitten: Rest up Hanky-pooh, I'm feeling feisty today
Me: Love you, see you later @ LS
SmittenKitten: The girls can't wait!

***

I arrive before she does at the rental house, we have been using for the last month to sneak away. I brought dinner tonight because I know she is running late. I start prepping the chicken I want to throw on the grill. Real men grill during the winter in the Midwest. We aren't pussies-- there isn't a season for grilling around here. It's a yearlong passion.

I open a bottle of red wine that I know she enjoys from the local winery and continue to prep the food. I grab the potatoes and chop them into bite-sized pieces, add some onion, and yellow and red peppers, then wrap it into a foil pouch with some salt, pepper, and garlic. I pull out the makings for a salad and hear the garage door open.

The door opens and I hear, "Hey babe, I'm sorry I was running late."

"Don't worry, get your coat off and come have a glass of wine while I finish putting dinner together."

She walks in and puts her arms around me and gives me a big kiss. "Hi."

"Hi, how was your day baby?"

"It was long but then my favorite boyfriend sent me the cutest candle and it made me smile. So, thank you. I loved it."

"I love my shirt. Can't wait to wear it."

"What's for dinner, and do you need any help?"

"Nope, let me spoil you a little bit tonight. Do you want a glass of wine? I opened your favorite red. Can I pour you a glass?"

"I'd love that. I have something fun we can do while you finish dinner. Let me grab it."

I pour her a glass of wine and grab a beer for myself while she pulls some cards out of her purse. "What's that?"

"It's a deck of Would You Rather cards. I thought it would be fun to do together and this seems like a perfect time."

"Okay, shoot."

She grabs the first card and asks, "Would you rather have the ability to see ten minutes into the future or 150 years into the future?"

"Easy, ten minutes."

"Why'd you pick that answer G?"

"Ten minutes seems to matter more. I'll be dead in 150 so it doesn't matter does it?"

"Probably right, I'd answer the same. Next card…Would you rather team up with Wonder Woman or Captain Marvel? I'd pick Wonder Woman. You?"

"Absolutely Wonder Woman, she's hot and I love my brunettes. Captain Marvel might zap me with her energy."

"Oh god, you are a dork. I forgot that you love your superhero movies so much."

"Hill, there is nothing sexier than a woman in a superhero costume."

"I'll remember that when I need to get you to bend my way. Next one…Would you rather have another 10 years with your partner or a one-night stand with your celebrity crush?"

"You, always you. I've waited way too long to have you as my partner to not have forever with you."

She stares at me with her mouth a bit open and her eyes looking a little shinier than usual. She quietly says, "Me too G."

"What's next," I ask.

"Would you rather have a personal maid or a personal chef?" I watch her smile get big and stretch across her face. "You better answer this the right way buddy."

"Hmm, not sure on this one. If I never have to clean another toilet, I may be okay with that." Her eyes are getting squinty, so I better save myself. "But…once you have a personal chef there is no turning back. I don't think I could ever give you up."

"Nice save mister," she says. "Would you rather spend a year at war or a year in prison? OH! Sorry G. We can skip that one."

"No, I'll answer. I'd rather spend a year at war, which I have because I want to make sure you and everyone I love are safe and have a future. I can't make that difference if I'm locked up."

She walks over and hugs me tight, "But no more mister. You put your time in, now it's time to be here safe and with me."

"Let me ask some of those goofy cards," I say and she hands me the deck. "Would you rather drink from a toilet or pee in a litter box?"

"That's gross. I'd pee in the damn box. No biggie," she says.

"I suppose I have already peed in a litter box when on duty."

"That you have, I'm sure."

"OH, this one is good, Hill…would you rather find a rat in your kitchen or a roach in your bed?"

She grabs the cards and puts them away, "Neither and that is the end of that. A rat in my kitchen. As if."

I laugh, kiss her nose, and grab the chicken. "Let me get the chicken on the grill so we can eat. Be right back."

I head to the deck where the grill is and I hear her mumbling to herself about a rat in her kitchen and what she would do to it. I smile and head to the grill. That's my woman. Talking about murdering a rat that doesn't exist.

Chapter Thirty-Four

Garrett

Hillary and I continue to spend time together as much as possible when our schedules allow, sharing time with friends separately and making them suffer with our ridiculous text messages back and forth about who's allowed to participate in group activities. They are continuing to humor us which we both find hilarious and entertaining. It's gotten to a point where we almost harass them with the back and forth. Cooper is on to us though, I can tell, but he won't question me or what is going on until he knows I'm ready to spill the details.

Since we are heading out of town for the weekend together, Hillary decided to drive over here and leave her car in my garage. We didn't want to leave her car at the rental since we were heading out of town and the house would be vacant. I have my car in the driveway so she can just pull right in and as soon as she gets here, we can go, so where is she?

I see lights flash as she pulls into the driveway about ten minutes late. I hear her shutting doors and then see the door into the house open.

"Sorry, I'm later than expected. At the last minute, I moved the catering van around to the back of my shop so that anyone driving by doesn't see it. You know, just in case, and then wonder why I am not at my event with my catering van."

"Hey baby, no worries. We have time. Tonight, we are just eating at the cabin and relaxing. I didn't make reservations except for breakfasts and the chef's dinner for our New Year's Eve celebration."

"That sounds perfect. I am exhausted because I tried to get caught up this week from all the holiday parties and closing out the books for the year. Once we head home on Sunday, I want to be able to focus on the new year and the new budget. Plus, Griffin caught me on my way out and wanted to know where you are taking me. I didn't tell him, but he will cover if anyone gets suspicious and wanted to let you know your shirt is ready for you."

"It's probably good that he is in on us and helping us with our secret getaway. Rob was harassing me about New Year's and having our traditional chili and cornbread gathering on New Year's Day but I told him I'm sick and can't leave the house. It was the only way to get him off my back and for him to accept that I wasn't going to be around after my shifts."

"Why is your brother such a pain in the ass," she says with a laugh. "I love him, but he loves to poke until he gets his way. You'd think he is the youngest and not Stella with the way he always has to win or have the last say."

"Middle child syndrome I suppose. Are you ready to head out baby? The sooner I have you to myself the better."

"Absolutely, let's get out of here. Do I have to lay low while we drive out of town?"

"Nah, just put your head in my lap until we leave town," I say with a wink.

"I don't think so mister, I haven't tested your ability to not crash while driving during a blow job."

"Wanna test it now?"

"No, I want to get to Galena and then get you naked safely in our cabin. Let's go!" She grabs my hand and drags me out of the house.

***

We arrived at the Inn just before eight o'clock that evening. During our check-in, they suggested we order dinner before the kitchen closes and they will deliver our meal right to the cabin tonight since we arrived later than expected.

Walking along the trail to the cabin Hillary keeps stopping and staring up into the night sky. "Wow, look at all the stars up there. You can tell that we left the city sky. I don't think I've ever seen so many.- It's beautiful." She brings her arms around me and squeezes, "Thank you for the romantic getaway, G."

"There sure are a lot. If you want, we can take a walk after we eat. They have a trail all the way down to the river. Seems like they have the walks cleared of any snow or ice."

"Let's do that. It's so bright out here under all these stars that it'd be a shame to miss it and afterward you can make sure to warm me up."

We make our way to the cabin, and she walks in ahead of me, "Oh my god G, look how cute this is."

I walk in behind her and look around the space. The cabin is not even six hundred square feet, but it does have a king-size bed, a small kitchen galley, a fireplace, and a two-person whirlpool tub. Cookies are sitting on a small table and fresh flowers are in a vase.

"Wow, this is so charming. I may not want to let you out of here for New Year's Eve tomorrow."

She walks over and lays across the bed and pats the mattress. "Come over here and relax," she says. "I bet we have about fifteen more minutes before our food arrives."

I lay down next to her and look over at her, "Are you happy, baby?"

Her smile lights up her face, "I am extremely happy and as soon as we eat you promised me a stroll under the stars."

I pull her into my chest and kiss her, "I'm going to give you that and then some baby. An entire weekend away and no one to bother us. I can't think of a better way to spend the time."

"Hmm, I agree. It's very beautiful here. Thank you for making the weekend special for me."

"For us, Hill. I will always make life special for us. I want you happy and trust me, this is only the beginning."

There's a knock on the door so our dinner must have arrived. I get up to help the delivery person and slip him a tip for running out in the cold for us. "Come on baby, let's eat so we can go walk around so you can count all the stars.

***

I hear my phone buzzing over on the nightstand. Hillary is still wrapped around me like a burrito sleeping because we barely slept last night being too busy enjoying each other's bodies. I close my eyes and try to relax and enjoy the moment, but my phone continues to buzz. I better make sure it's not an emergency.

I kiss her temple, "Baby I need to grab my phone. It won't stop going off."

She kisses my chest, "Okay, make sure we order our breakfast and enjoy that two-person soaker tub over there."

"Sounds like a great idea." I grabbed my phone and see some text messages from Rob.

Rob: Hope you are feeling ok

Rob: Heard you are sick

Rob: Mom made you some soup

Me: That was nice of her to do. I will get it tomorrow when I feel better

Rob: What's wrong with you? Flu?

Me: Yeah, think so

Me: Just staying in bed trying to live through it

Rob: K-say hi to Hilly for me

Me: Will do

"FUCK!"

I look over at Hillary and she has a worried look on her face. "What's the matter G, is everyone okay? It's not Bree and the baby, is it?"

"Nope, just my jackass brother and he knows we are together."

"What? How?"

Me: Why do you think I'm w Hill???

Rob: I'm in your house dumbass dropping off mom's soup and her car is in the garage *winky emoji* Is she your smitten kitten? Otherwise, I am confused.
Me: Yes, and keep it to yourself
Rob: Happy4U. Mums the word but I want deets later!!!
Me: No. keep it quiet
Rob: 10-4 good buddy *winking emoji* *heart emoji*

"Jesus! He dropped off Mom's soup since I told everyone I'm sick. He then saw your car in my garage and put it together," I told her.

"Two down a bunch to go," she says. "It's fine. At least I know Rob is scared of me, so he won't spill the beans. I'm surprised we were able to keep things under their radar this long."

"I know but I like that we didn't have to answer questions with everyone while we were finding our way. It's going to be bad enough when we do come clean."

"Nah, I figure we just have to do it with a big announcement," she says. "You know how much I like to be the center of attention.

Chapter Thirty-Five

Hillary

There is nothing I love more than waking up with Garrett in bed with me. His size and his ability to make me feel safe and cherished aren't things I've ever felt before with a man. Knowing that Garrett waited for me to get my head out of my ass and stuck around while he got the tiger side of my personality puts him at the top of my list. He witnessed and felt the beasty side of me, and he still wants to be a big part of my life. If that shit didn't scare him away, then he may not be able to spook. Interesting and call me one lucky bitch for sure!

Rob woke us up this morning with his usual trickster personality and of course, Garrett being half asleep let the cat out of the bag. Oh well, eventually the others will learn our little secret but if we can keep it on the down low a little bit longer…because not having the pressure of the girls wanting to hear every little detail yet…keeps it special and just us. This is our moment—finding ourselves and what this could potentially mean. I mean come on, who would ever want to give up this amazing sex, and can we just pause for a moment and think about Garrett and his body? He's so strong with all those muscles and those tattoos down his shoulder and arm, his beautiful abs that I love to run my tongue along, and the bullseye of his cock that knows exactly how to trigger my fantastic orgasms. When he holds me in his arms and wraps around me with his thighs—a girl couldn't die in a better fantasy.

"Baby, what do you want to do today? Now that we have had our delicious waffles and strawberries and I've had my way with you in that bath and here in this bed. Do you want to go wander the grounds or we can take a little drive into Galena and see the shops?"

"Mmm, is it bad if I don't find the option of you putting clothes on favorable?"

"No, I am happy to stay naked and let you have your way with me but I think it would be great to go take a walk today and see the grounds since it was already dark when we got here. I know they have some nice walking trails."

He kisses my nose and smiles. "Okay, I suppose I can let you out of my bed for a little bit today. When is our dinner reservation?"

"We need to be at dinner at eight o'clock and then it's a seven-course chef's dinner. After dinner, they have some live music and dancing until our New Year countdown with champagne."

"That sounds amazing. I can't wait until you see the dress I brought to make you suffer through the night."

"Aw Hill, you continue to surprise me with how sweet you can be."

"Just trying to keep you on your toes and I don't want you to get bored with me G."

He grabs my chin and forces me to look at him, "Baby, I could never be bored with you. You are a crazy and feisty woman and that will never change. That is one thing that I love about you."

"My feistiness?"

"Yes, that and that you continue to keep me on my toes and fight for whatever you want. I don't think that part of you will ever change. You have a fire in your belly and it's hot. Turns me the fuck on all the time."

"You say the sweetest things to me."

"Now, get your sexy ass up and throw on some warm clothes. We are going out on an adventure and then we can come to get ready for dinner. I want to show you off a little bit. We can grab a late lunch at the restaurant. When we checked in, I saw that they have a fire pit outside and provide smores fixings."

"Oh, that sounds delicious. Let's do that!"

***

Garrett and I walked all over the grounds and along the river throughout the day. Most of it was frozen but there were some sections where the water was flowing. It was cold out on the grounds but with the snow and the shimmer from the sun, it felt warmer than it was. We had a delicious late lunch of roast beef sandwiches and potato soup. After lunch, we sat at the fire pit and made smores with some of the other guests. All couples from around the area like us. It was so nice not to have that feeling of hiding in plain sight. We were just a normal couple having a romantic weekend away for the holiday, the same as the others. When asked how long we have been together or how we met, Garrett proudly shared we have known each other since we were in elementary school, and it took until recently for him to prove he was the one meant for me. The big sap, but my inner girly feelings were screaming *aww*. Some of the other women whispered *lucky girl* and *he's a keeper* to me- I completely agree with them.

Garrett leans into my side, "Baby I think we need to go take a nap before we get ready for the New Year."

I look at his face and see the wickedness in his eyes. "Nap huh? You don't look very tired to me."

"So, so tired," he says with a wink.

"I'm ready whenever you are so lead the way."

He stands abruptly, "It's been great meeting all of you today, Hill and I are going to go rest up for the late evening. See you all later."

"Nice to meet all of you," I say to the couples around the fire.

We walk hand in hand to the cabin as he hands me two marshmallows and a big piece of chocolate, "What's this?"

"I want to eat smores off you. I saw we have a microwave."

"You are crazy G."

"Why? Because I want to lick melted chocolate and marshmallow off your body. That's not crazy, that is delicious."

"Whatever you want babe, I'm game. Just don't get the bed sticky."

"Aw Hilly, are you doubting my tongue's ability?"

"No, that is something I never have to worry about…well…only if you don't lick me enough."

Laughing we headed into the cabin and started pulling off our clothes together.

***

"Babe, you need to let me out of bed so I can shower and get ready for tonight."

"No, not yet baby. I'm so comfortable right now."

"Garrett, you are laying across my boobs with your hand between my legs. I'm so glad you are comfy but I need to go shower and start getting ready for our date."

His head pops up and I see a big smile spread across his face, "We are going on a date. On New Year's Eve. I think this is the first time in my life I kissed the girl of my dreams at midnight. You have some big shoes to fill so don't screw it up."

"Get off me jackass. I could say the same back to you! How many toads I have kissed at midnight? So, so, many."

"All right, I get the message. Let me just kiss them goodbye quick." He moves to kiss and lick my breasts.

"You are ridiculous but continue. That feels good."

He stops and looks up into my eyes, "So good you don't have to get up yet?"

"No, I want to look beautiful for you and I need time to get ready. We've been in bed for hours already. Don't be so selfish."

"Okay baby, I won't be selfish. Go take your shower."

***

192

I showered and paid special attention to applying lotion to my body afterward. I found some sparkly lotion that doesn't have a flavor, so I generously apply that to my cleavage before I put on my black lace bustier, garter, and stockings. I am wearing a silver mini dress with long sheer puff sleeves, a deep V-neckline, and a curve-hugging silhouette, this dress is perfect for tonight and paired with my red strappy heels-I am a walking sex kitten! I wear my hair in big curls that fall around my face and paint on smokey eyes. I keep my lips nude but with a shimmer. I want to be able to make out with my man and not give him a lipstick face. Garrett is waiting in the main room while I finished primping in the bathroom. Here goes, deep breath, I open the door and walk into the room. He's standing with a glass of bourbon looking at the fire in the room. He hears the door open and turns to me.

"My God Hill, you are stunning." I watch him look at me up and down and then again up and down. He slowly walks towards me. "I am one lucky son of a bitch. Jesus, I don't think I have ever seen something more beautiful. Thank you."

"Thank you?"

"Yes, thank you," he says. "For being my woman and not some other asshole." He kisses my lips gently, "I love you."

He loves me. I've waited my whole life for a wonderful man like this to tell me he loves me. I love him too. "I love you too."

"You are absolutely beautiful, and I can't wait to dance the night away with you and kiss you at midnight."

"Thank you, now back up a moment so I can stare at your handsomeness because it isn't often, I get to see you in a suit. My oh my, aren't you a handsome fella? You know you turn me on when you are in a uniform, but G… I must say, you in a suit and all cleaned up is mighty tasty. Especially because I know what you have hiding underneath. You look very handsome, and you are going to make all the other men envious. Oh, how fun! Let's go make all the other couples jealous of how good we look together!"

"And…there she is." Laughing he helps me with my coat, and we walk to dinner holding hands. "Be careful not to fall on your ass in those come fuck me shoes."

"My what?" I am giggling because that right there tells me this outfit hit home. "Come fuck me shoes? Is that all I need to do to get you excited?"

"No, I just have to think about you, but this look tonight baby, I am going to be hard all night."

"Poor baby, well I better not tell you about the sexy things I'm wearing for you underneath."

I hear him groan and squeeze me tighter as we continue to walk. Me having a grin from one ear to the other. I love this man and his need for me. That ladies is how a man should make you feel truly wanted. Like they can't breathe without you. That is how this wonderful man makes me feel and I am not ever living without it again.

***

The restaurant is beautifully lit with candles and magical twinkling lights for the holidays. Our seven-course chef's meal was simply delicious, and we are now holding each other on the dance floor and enjoying the live music.

"I love this night. Can we have dance parties like this even after the night is over G?"

"If it means I get to hold you in my arms, run my hands up and down you, and pretend to be dancing, then yes. I will even hang a disco ball in the house if that is necessary."

"We should tell Julia to have dancing events occasionally at her Harte of Harmony. We could charge tickets to cover the cost of a musician and it would give us some fun adult nights like going to prom. OH! We could even do theme nights. I mean if she has this event venue and I

194

am the town caterer there really isn't a reason that we can't throw our own parties like that and invite the town."

"Sounds great, but that means we have to tell everyone about us because I am never watching you dance or be held by another man again. You. Are. Mine. I don't share baby."

"You better not fucking think I will share you. Have you had too much bourbon tonight? You, crazy man. You know once a man hits my bed, I don't share myself or allow him to wander. That's just silly talk. I do think we need to let them all know our secret, but let's just see if Rob can keep his mouth closed a bit longer and enjoy this secret love affair a little longer."

"Everyone, we have a few minutes before the midnight countdown. The staff are walking around the room with glasses of champagne. Please grab your glass and whomever you plan to kiss at midnight," the Inn owner says to the room. "Thank you for sharing New Year's Eve with us here at the Inn. May your New Year be filled with Love, Happiness, and Laughter."

"I love you, Hillary Greene."

"I love you, Garrett Stone."

"Ten, nine, eight, seven, six, five, four, three, two, one…HAPPY NEW YEAR!"

Chapter Thirty-Six

Garrett

I'm hosting a long overdue poker night with the guys later and I'm looking forward to it. I haven't seen the guys too often lately, especially with Hill and I taking our turns and messing with the whole gang. I'm about to head to lunch when Jilly knocks and pokes her head into my office.

"Hey Sheriff, you've got another delivery. Did you tell your lady friend to make sure I can't snoop? These deliveries lately are mighty tough to try to get details from. She even sent this one wrapped up in smiley face paper."

"Jilly, why do you feel you have the okay to look through my deliveries?"

"Pure entertainment Sheriff. We are all just taking bets about who she is and when we are going to see her walk through the door. Do you know Katie started a pool? We have dates and what she looks like. It's been great! Even got the fire department involved."

"Wait...what?"

"Aw, it's nothing, Sheriff. We're all just so happy to see you happy. It's so nice to see you walking around with that big 'ol smile across your face. Joe even caught you whistling when you get coffee in the kitchen. That's on the pool too."

"My coffee breaks?"

"No sir, the whistling."

"Jilly, thanks for the delivery. Go head on back to reception please."

"You got it, Sheriff. Hope it's a nice surprise today in that box."

I grab the wrapped gift and open it. I did tell Hillary to make sure that her notes and gifts were more discreet since my employees seem to think it's okay to snoop. I pulled out the handwritten note from her.

I'm not flirting with you. I'm just trying to make you horny. Xoxo Smitten Kitten…meow

I looked inside the box and there is a scratch card and a penny. The card says *Are You Getting Lucky Tonight? (Of course!)*
Scratch me- get 3 of a kind to win. I take the penny and start to scratch off all the hidden areas. I begin to see Butt Stuff, Blow Job, 69, Role Play, Striptease, and Anal. Lucky me I get three of a kind, twice!

Me: I hope you are ready to deliver my prize
SmittenKitten: What did you get *winking emoji*
Me: My favorite plus Striptease
SmittenKitten: Ohh, you are one lucky man indeed
Me: Tomorrow? Since I have poker tonight
SmittenKitten: As soon as I have you in my sites
Me: Not soon enough
Me: Oh hey, did you know police/fire depts have a pool going about me
SmittenKitten: Yep, I put my money on you! Don't let me down.
Me: Wait what? You bet on us? LOL
SmittenKitten: Oh yeah sweet cheeks and I plan to win.
Me: Isn't that cheating?
SmittenKitten: not if you don't know what I bet on *winking emoji*
SmittenKitten: Love you *kissing emoji*
Me: Love you more

***

I'm home throwing some chips in a bowl when Rob knocks and walks into my house, "Hey big guy….so….getting it on with Hilly."

"Knock it off and keep it quiet."
"It's true?"

198

"Yes, but we would like to keep it quiet for now. We're hoping to avoid outside comments just like when you waltzed in here just now."

"Nah, I've got you but is this for real or just scratching an itch because if it's just scratching an itch there are safer chicks to have gone to for that."

"Rob, I'm going to say this one time and one time only. It's serious—for both of us and if you ever refer to her in that way again, you and me, we're going to have a serious problem."

He backs away from me in a surrender pose with a big smile across his face, "I hear you, man. Serious huh…am I going to be your best man?"

I scrub my hand over my face, "Please drop it before the guys get here. When there's more to tell you, I promise you will be the second one I come to."

"Cool…What! Second? Ah I see, I'm just the little brother, your brother-in-arms comes first."

"Do you want me to tell you at the same time? Will that make you feel better?"

"Yes, Garrett. Yes, it would. I expect to be told at the same time as Cooper."

"Jesus, you exhaust me."

"I wouldn't want it any other way, bro. Where's the beer?"

"Fridge, go help yourself."

Finally, the rest of the guys start arriving to spare me from any more little brother harassment. The last one to arrive is Jackson looking like he just came from the office. Rubbing my hands together I say to my buddies, "Who's ready to lose some money!"

Chapter Thirty-Seven

Hillary

Lately, it seems the girls and I haven't had our Saturday mornings free to meet at Harmonious Bites which is Ellen's cute little coffee shop. Since I missed New Year's Eve with the gang, the girls demanded we all schedule this time into our weekend morning.

I arrived early since Garrett and I spent last night together. Knowing it was going to be an early morning he got up early to go for a workout today with Jackson. I'm already drinking my hazelnut latte when Julia comes rushing in wearing running gear.

"Did you run here?"

"Yes, I have been sitting a lot this week and figured I would get some exercise in, but I didn't realize how cold it would be this morning," she says.

"Jules, it's January in Illinois. Of course, it's cold. Did your nipples freeze and fall off or are they still attached?"

"Shut up Hill, so what's new with you? I feel like I never see you anymore."

"I'm good. Busy. Work is good."

"That's it? No update for me on your love life?"

"What love life?" *Shit. Did Rob already spill the beans?*

"The last I heard you were seeing some handyman or something and seemed to be enjoying him. Is that over?"

"Oh, Hank. No, I still see him when I can. Work was busy though with all the holiday parties."

"Is it getting serious? You don't seem to keep them around long enough for us to meet them. Are we going to ever meet this one?"

"I'll think about it," I say trying to keep a straight face. If you only knew I'm dating your brother Jules. I look up in time to see Bree coming in with the help of Sam. Sam has a worried look on her face and they march right over to our table.

"Hey girls, I'm going to sit Bree down right here while I go grab our coffees," Sam says. "Make sure you keep her here."

"What the hell is going on," I ask.

Sam looks at Bree with a stern face, "Bree just about fell on her ass outside by trying to climb over a frozen snow pile next to the parking lot. Sit," she points at Bree, "Don't move, I will get your decaf latte."

Julia grabs Bree's hand, "Oh no, are you okay? Did you hurt yourself?"

Looking extremely guilty Bree says, "I'm okay. I was trying to save time by going over the little snow pile instead of walking all the way around to the sidewalk. I may have slipped since it was icy and when my arms started flapping Sam came running and screaming and grabbed ahold of me. It was more bad judgment and embarrassment on my part than anything else," Bree says.

Julia holds her hand, "Bree, please don't take stupid chances like that. It's bad enough to slip on ice that you don't see but I'd hate to hear you fell because you felt you were in a hurry or taking a shortcut. Noah would have a heart attack if anything happened to you or the baby."

"I know, I promise I will make better choices. It's not just me anymore. I have some news to share with everyone but let's wait until Sam and Ellen can come to sit with us."

"Is this good news," I ask.

"Yes, baby news," Bree says with a glow on her face.

Sam and Ellen come back to our table with the drinks and a plate of scones and muffins. Once they sit and we all have a sweet baked good to enjoy Bree gets a big smile on her face.

"Now that all my best friends are sitting here, I can share some exciting news with you." She takes a big breath and says, "We just found out we are having a baby boy!"

We all give our congratulations and get up and give her big hugs. "Bree I am so happy for you. Oh my God,

202

Noah must be over the moon with excitement about having a son," Ellen says.

"He is so excited! He is going to drive around today and find all the guys to hand out cigars."

"Isn't that what you do when the baby is born," I ask.

"Yes, but this is a practice run he said."

"Either way, that is wonderful news. I am so excited for both of you. Now you can focus on your names," Julia adds.

"Now that we know the baby is going to be a boy, we named him. His name is going to be Jameson Scott Roarke. Noah and I picked out Jameson because he loves his whiskey and Scott was my grandpa's name on my mom's side."

"I love his name," Sam says.

Ellen asks, "Great name, sounds strong and brave. Are you going to call him Jameson or give him a nickname?"

"We are going to call him Jameson, as a teacher I don't want to shorten his name to something else. He should grow up to be proud of the name he was given. Noah feels the same."

"I agree, plus that is an awesome name," I say.

"We are both so excited. He is growing big and strong in my belly and so far, everything is going as planned. He is due during summer break, so I won't have to miss any work. Right now, I am planning on going back to work, but the more Noah tells me I could be a stay-at-home mom, the more I kind of think I like the idea. I am having this baby a little older than usual and I don't know if we will have more so missing anything would be horrible."

Julia hugs her, "You could always be a substitute if you want to stay home but still have your hand in teaching. Don't make a final decision now. You will have the summer home with him for the first couple of months after he is born. You don't have to give your decision to the school now do you?"

"No, I have until the end of my maternity leave to let Diane know whether I will come back to teaching

Kindergarten full time, but I don't want to leave them in a lurk at the last minute. If Jameson is on time according to his due date, I would be due to go back to school at the start of the new year."

"Bree, you have time. Just enjoy this pregnancy and the first couple of months of loving him. Just promise no more stupid shit like climbing frozen mountains of snow. Jesus. I think you about gave Sam a heart attack," I say.

"Yes, she did," Sam replies. "Thank God I was just crossing the street and watched her debate her route and I ran because I wanted to make sure she didn't fall on her butt."

"I am so sorry Sam. I promise I won't try going over snow and ice anymore. I didn't mean to scare everyone."

"Enough about making Bree feel bad. How was everyone's New Year? Sorry, I had to miss it because of work."

"It was fun. Since you were gone, Garrett was down with the flu or something, and Bree and Noah ended up staying home. The rest of us had a nice dinner at our house and a champagne toast at midnight, and then everyone went on their way home. It's not like it used to be when we were in our twenties and didn't care how hungover or tired, we were the next day. Rob made a big pot of chili and cornbread and Jackson, and I stopped by his place with the kids on New Year's Day with Mom and Dad," Julia says.

"Sorry, I missed it. Work. Always work," I say trying to keep a straight face.

"Sorry we ditched out on you guys, but Noah and I had washed the bedding and some of the baby clothes that morning, and I was exhausted. We both laid down for an afternoon nap and by the time we woke up, we were too lazy to get dressed and head out. We ended up just making a simple dinner and snuggling on the couch watching New York and the ball drop. We laughed at midnight because we figured with a baby, we probably won't be able to stay up late enough for a couple of years to watch the ball drop."

"You are right about that," Julia says. "When Daniel and Josie were little, we started celebrating New Year's Eve at eight o'clock with dessert from dinner with the kids. Then we were all in bed by probably ten o'clock. Now that the kids are older, they either stay up or they just don't care and go to bed. It's funny how things change as your life priorities change."

"Being an adult is hard," I say while laughing. "Woe is me and having to stay up late. When we were kids and had our sleepovers, we could stay up all night. Now as an adult, if I'm in bed with a sexy man and having sexy times all night I feel like a zombie the next day, just to repeat it all the next night."

"Hmm," Sam says. "Let's talk about those sexy times Hilly. What's up with your love life these days? Last book club you were into someone. Is that still a thing?"

I look around the table at my best friends and only Julia knows the current news, or at least the news of Hank. Without a big bold-out lie to my best friends, I seem to be on the spot of needing to share some details. "I am still seeing him. We both have busy work schedules, so we have to make time to fit it into our weeks, but we manage to see each other at least every week. He is good to me and knows his way around the bedroom and Hillary-land, but for once I think I found someone that is charming and also appreciates me. We are taking it slow and getting to know each other." My friends are all perched and leaning toward me like it's Storytime at the library. "What?" They all look at each other with smirks then back at me. "Seriously, what? You are all starting to look a bit creepy."

"You were glowing just now Hilly. It was like a moment in one of my romance stories. You like him, don't you," Bree asks.

"I don't hate him."

"Oh my, ladies, we need to remember this moment because I don't think we've seen this side of Hilly since the eighth grade when Hilly when was in love with Jeffrey

Michaels and swore she would die when he broke her heart after the dance," Sam says.

"Yeah, you may be right," Bree agrees. "She is smitten, isn't she? I love this for you Hilly and you deserve to find someone that treats you right."

"Enough you dorks. I like him, yes. He knows how to satisfy me and make me feel special. Let's not get carried away with anything else. I don't want to get myself hoping for something if it doesn't happen."

"How does he feel? Have you asked him," Ellen asks.

"I think he feels the same way that I do."

"I love this! I am happy that you are happy Hill," Julia says. "When do we get to meet him?"

"Not yet, we are still seeing where this goes. I don't want to go there yet so give us some time."

Chapter Thirty-Eight

Garrett

Mondays have become my least favorite day of the week because by noon I seem to be going through withdrawal from having Hillary with me. We spent the weekend at our love shack as Hill loves to call it. She made us do a taste test challenge which at times was disgusting. The shit that she thinks of to make sure we know each other as well as possible. How determining the best-tasting mayonnaise or peanut butter could save our lives in a hostage situation is anyone's guess but Hillary seemed to think it was important. She had various brands of mayo, peanut butter, cheese, potato chips, ice cream, and whiskey for us to sample. We went through each and picked our favorite. Again, why this was an important fact-finding mission is anyone's guess but to Hill, it was important so of course, I went along with the entire process. My stomach did not agree.

She should be receiving her delivery from Hank soon, so I have my phone ready. I'm sitting here in my office just waiting because I know she is in the shop doing inventory with Griffin and she will be there when her delivery arrives. I suppose in the meantime, I can work on making next month's schedule for who's on duty.

SmittenKitten: hmm….you sent me a rabbit
Me: It's a very special rabbit…his ears will tickle your clit
SmittenKitten: I know-thank you
Me: You know???
SmittenKitten: Yes, I just spent 30 minutes in my office….alone…with Bob

And I'm hard as stone. Holy shit, she just used the vibrator in her office. Wait, who the fuck is Bob?

SmittenKitten: Bob was amazing. Thank you love for thinking of me. This sure takes the pressure off

Me: Who the fuck is Bob?

SmittenKitten: *laughing emoji* my rabbit. Battery. Operated. Buddy…BOB.

Me: I was about to go arrest some Bob's ass baby. Don't do that. Not when I think you have a guy chasing your pleasure that isn't me

SmittenKitten: Simmer down G. You know I love you but seeing as this bunny was a gift, I thought it was to use whenever I needed a little pick me up and your beautiful cock wasn't available *lips emoji*

Me: Maybe I didn't think this gift through. Yes, I want you to use it, but I was hoping I could participate

SmittenKitten: You want his ears to tickle your balls? I can help make that happen

Me: Not what I meant

SmittenKitten: Might feel good??

Me: Stop

SmittenKitten: We will explore later when you aren't still fired up thinking I was here naked with Bob

Me: Were you naked with the bunny?

SmittenKitten: Easier to play with my nipples that way *winky emoji*

Me: Jesus, Where's Griff

SmittenKitten: Kitchen

Me: You were naked and playing with yourself with Griff in the kitchen????????????

SmittenKitten: Yes sir

Me: HILL!!!!

SmittenKitten: He saw the gift, so I told him to put earbuds in and go away

Me: OMG you are killing me right now

SmittenKitten: Careful with gift giving then. What did you expect? Your cock is too far away and the bunny made me curious

Me: You baby, are a nut. Was the bunny good?

SmittenKitten: He was very good, but you babe are much MUCH better *winky emoji* LOVE YOU

Me: LOVE YOU 2

SmittenKitten: I have a meeting at 4:30 w a new client @ coops. Meet me there after?

Me: Coops? He doesn't know about us. Do you want me to tell him?

SmittenKitten: He's your BFF, go ahead-in secret...shh

Me: Love you...thank you.

SmittenKitten: *Heart emoji* Don't want him pissed because Rob knows first

Me: All good baby. See you there.

***

I walk into Coops around five o'clock still in uniform, because I am trying to keep my usual routine for appearance's sake. Coop does a double take when I slide into my normal seat at the end of the bar.

"Well, look who it is. I thought maybe you got tired of paying rent for that seat."

"Hey man, sorry I haven't been by lately. When I'm not working, I've been spending my free time with someone."

"Yeah, that part I know. It's the who that I am not sure about." Gesturing to the corner, "Hill is over at the table in the corner with a guy. Do you know what that is about? I can't tell if it's another one of her bad dates or a client. There have been a couple of times that he has touched her, and it looked a bit more intimate."

"WHAT!" I spin so fast and stand up to look over but hear Cooper laughing behind me.

"I guess that answers the who. Sit down big guy, just calling your bluff. Why don't I get you a soda since you are in uniform, and you tell me how long you've been seeing Hillary."

Before I sit down Hill glances over. She must have seen my idiot reaction to Coop just now, and she has a worried look on her face. I wink at her and see her face relax so I sit back down.

"That was dirty Coop. You know I don't keep secrets from you but this one, well, we decided to keep it a secret from everyone. At least for a little bit. We didn't want to make a big deal unless it was something that became bigger."

"And has it," Coop asks.

"Yeah. I love her."

"If you think after all these years of you sitting here stalking her bad dates and being miserable watching her from a distance, I wasn't aware of you being in love with her then you are the bigger idiot, not me buddy. Man, you were in love with her when I met you. So, how did you finally get her to talk to you and see things your way?"

"When we were stuck at the cabin, I tried talking to her, but it wouldn't happen. She avoided me like the plague. I wrote her a letter and slipped it under the door. She wrote me back still chewing me out about what went wrong and that's when I realized how badly I fucked things up with her. I ate crow man. I apologized in detail for what I did, what I thought, and how we misunderstood each other and our reactions. Then I came right out and told her I was in love with her."

"Brought the big guns out to play, didn't ya? She ran into your arms and hasn't left since?"

"No, it wasn't that easy. This is Hillary we are talking about. We talked things through finally and talked about what we wanted moving forward. I told her how I felt and that I wanted to explore my feelings for her and asked if she had any feelings for me. When she said yes, but wanted to keep it a secret, I thought she was up to something again." I look over at Cooper and I see his hesitation with that thought too. "I know, another fake truce, but it isn't."

"So, what's with all this bullshit about only one of you being in group situations at a time? I don't quite see the connection here."

"That was the part I was hesitant about because we are lying a bit to everyone, but as Hillary and I discussed seeing where our feelings could go, we also thought about interference from everyone. We thought what they don't know won't hurt them or interfere with trying to see if the two of us as a couple have enough to make it."

Coop pauses and looks me in the eye, like the soldier he is, "And does it? It is solid?"

I sit back, relax my shoulders that I have tensed up, "Yes, we've both said I love you, we are rarely apart, and I am planning on putting a ring on her finger."

Coop is just looking at me with his soldier glare and I can't read what he's thinking. "All right then, it's about damn time. Honestly, I think the two of you were made for each other. You will never get bored being with Hillary because she is going to keep you on your toes until the day you take your last breath and she needs someone that won't be afraid of her challenging personality."

"Coop, now be careful what you say about my future wife."
We both started to laugh and he gave me a high five. "I'm happy for you brother."

"Thanks, one more thing…you don't know about us and this arrangement. We don't want to tell anyone else yet. You, Rob, and Griff know. That's it. They found out accidentally, you I am telling."

"I got your back man. Though, I'm happy for you both, and be ready because your wife just ended her meeting and is coming this way with a determined look on her face."

Hillary leans against the bar next to me, "Hey Coop, did G fill you in on all the sexy times we are having," Hillary loudly whispers across the bar.

"Yes he did, but you aren't making it too secret right now," Coop answers with a chuckle.

"Well, he sent me a bunny today and it got me thinking about him all day long, so if you boys have had enough conversation I'd like to take my man back to our love shack and have my way with him. He agreed to try out some kinky lovemaking with Bob."

Coop's gaze lands on me with a raised brow, "Hill, let's go."

"Wait a sec…you care to elaborate on that Hill?" Lifting his hands in surrender, "No, as a matter of fact, I don't want to know. Bye, you two, have fun with Bob," Coop says with a snicker.

"Come on Hill, before you make me look like a bigger ass in front of my best friend."

She leans over the counter to Coop and whispers behind her hand-yet loud enough for me to hear, "It's my new vibrator he wants to try with me."

I grab her hand, "And…we are leaving."

We walk out of there still hearing Cooper laughing behind the bar. I can't even turn around to look at him and I already dread the next time I see him. We walked out of the restaurant and over to her car. "Woman, you are in trouble. You better get yourself to the house, be naked, and wait for me with your rabbit."

She leans in to kiss my cheek, "Honey, Bob and I will be wet and ready for your pleasure. See you there." She jumps in her car and smiles at me.

Chapter Thirty-Nine

Garrett

The week has dragged on but it's finally the weekend. Hill has no events and it's all quiet on the friend front. I am looking forward to staying in and enjoying a quiet weekend alone as a couple. We can enjoy the hot tub and then nap naked during the day. Maybe we make this a naked weekend?

Jilly pokes her around my semi-closed office door, "Knock, knock, Sheriff." In a sing-song voice, she says, "You have a special delivery."

"Come on in Jilly. You can put it down on my desk. I am just finishing up some paperwork before I head out for the weekend."

"Good plans this weekend?"

"For once I am going to stay in and relax all weekend. I hope we don't have any emergencies that force me to put my uniform on. I'm tired and I just need a couple of days to relax and watch the idiot box. What about you? Fun plans with the family and kids?"

"I'm taking the whole lot to a bounce place filled with inflatables. It's too dang cold for the little ones to be outside so I am packing them all up and letting them exhaust themselves inside a bunch of blown-up houses. Hopefully, they have enough staff so we adults can just relax and watch."

"They didn't have anything like that when I was a kid. That sounds like almost as much fun as Disney World. I hope they have fun and wear themselves out for you."

"So, another special delivery. What do you get in these surprises anyway?"

"Jilly, are you trying to cheat on the betting board?"

"No, I am just as curious as a cat."

"Well, if they were meant to be shared, I would tell ya, but they aren't. Just some fun surprises."

"Fine, you enjoy your gift and then get on home. The temps are dropping fast, and you've been here enough this week."

"You and Katy get out as soon as your shifts are over too. Be careful on the ice and snow."

"Will do Sheriff. See you Monday."

Let's see what she sent today. I open the wrapped gift and there are a couple of individually wrapped items. I look for a card and don't see one until I notice there's a small note taped to the wrapped gift. I pulled it off and read *Playtime never tasted so good xoxo meow*. I open the wrapped box and find Erotic Lover's Chocolate Paint. Shaking my head and smiling so big it hurts I grab the next item and pull off the card. This one reads *Dear Hanky, There's a saying that I think fits this gift perfectly…If you liked it then you shoulda put a ring on it…and we will. Xoxo SmittenKitten & Beyonce.* I open the box and individual little packets of candy or something fall onto my desk. What the heck did she send me? I grab one of the little packets and look at it and realize that she sent me a bunch of hot pink cock rings that vibrate called the Screaming Orgasm Maker. Oh lord, does she think she is putting my dick in a vice? Grabbing my phone, I sent out a text to her.

Me: Got your delivery
Me: Not sure about this one Hilly
SmittenKitten: You will love it
Me: Have you used one before?
SmittenKitten: No, but you liked BOB and this is much MUCH better for you…and me at the same time
Me: Not sure it will fit
SmittenKitten: Your ginormous cock will fit and we can ride the Screaming Orgasm Maker together
Me: Okay
SmittenKitten: It's supposed to make you harder, last longer, and give you a killer orgasm like NEVER before
Me: Chocolate Paint looks good-can't wait to cover you head to toe

SmittenKitten: We needed toys to use for our long weekend in
SmittenKitten: I can't wait to put a ring on it *winking emoji*
SmittenKitten: I also plan on painting your body and licking it clean
Me: You first, you are already sweet but this may be even sweeter
SmittenKitten: Love you-see you soon
Me: Love You Too
SmittenKitten: Don't forget potato salad *smiling emoji*
Me: *thumbs up emoji*

Everyone is keeping warm at home during this cold Midwest January. Hill asked me to grab her some of Gertie's potato salad so we can hibernate all weekend so that is why I find myself on a Friday after work standing in the 1-Stop General store being observed by our town gossip.

"Happy Friday Gertie. Any fun plans this weekend?"

"Oh Sheriff, the only thing I plan on doing other than working here a few hours is staying home and watching that new Rom-Com that Jax and Sophie are in. It finally came out on cable so I may bunge it all weekend."

"You mean binge?"

"Yes, that's what I said, I'm going to bunge it all weekend. I saw it when it hit the theater but I am so proud of my nephew so I try to watch his movies as much as possible and increase the views for him."

"I'm not sure that's how it works, but I hope you enjoy yourself. Do you have that big container of your potato salad I asked you to put away for me?"

"I sure do sheriff. What do you need so much for? Is someone having a dinner party?"

"Nope, I'm off this weekend and we just want to stay in and eat good food. Hill requested some of your potato salad."

"Oh. OH! Is Hillary the one that puts happiness in your step? Our own Miss Greene? Isn't that lovely? Oh, how I love all you kids so much and to think two of our own have found love and happiness together."

Shit. How is it I put my foot in my mouth here of all places? I must be tired, but I better fix this quickly. "Miss Gertie, now I promise to share some gossip if YOU promise to keep it quiet and not post anything about it. Can you do that for me please?"

"Sherriff, I will do anything you ask. Now spill."

"Yes, Hillary and I are seeing each other but no one knows. Not even our friends or family because before we made it public we wanted to make sure it was something real. So, if you can keep this little bit of information to yourself we would both be very appreciative."

Her eyes are lighting up and she's running her hands together so happy to be in on our secret. She leans forward and whispers, "I am so happy for you both. I always thought you'd end up with one of those pretty girls, but you never made your move. I've been watching you fall all over yourself around Hillary though since you came home from your service time and I think she's a good match for you. Your secret is safe with me. You will let me know when I can share it though right?"

"You will be the first to know! Now stay warm and be careful out there with the ice and snow."

"You to Sheriff, have a nice snuggle-down."

I walk to my cruiser and sit down inside where it's warm. How in the hell did that just happen? Of all people to not have my guard up around but maybe it's time for this news to not be so secret anymore. Just in case I better check Harmony Hears. Gertie usually moves fast on her gossip posts on Facebook.

<u>STAY HOME-OUT OF THE COLD-SHERIFF APPROVED</u>

Even our own Sherriff Stone just came by to order a big batch of my delicious potato salad in hopes to stay home and out of the cold this weekend. I think that's a great idea! If anyone needs to stock up on supplies before you snuggle down and bunge movies, stop in at the 1-Stop General Store. The Sheriff says to watch the ice and snow!

Chapter Forty

Hillary

This winter cold is getting ridiculous. I am so cold down to the bones and all I want to do is crawl back into bed. Unfortunately, I am at work and going through supplies to finish up the big order for an event at Julia's Harte of Harmony this weekend. She is hosting a bride and groom renewing their vows. Must be great to have someone that you love so much you want to renew your commitment in front of all the people you love. If I could have that once I'd take it.

My phone rings, "Hello, A Matter of Taste, Hillary speaking."

"Hilly it's Jules. I just got a call from the winery. I worked with them on customizing labels for this renewal this weekend. Would you or Griffin be able to go over there and pick up a couple of cases we will be serving, or should I see if Jackson can help me get all of them?"

"We can handle it. I will take the van over and get the wine and then I can drop it off in the kitchen there. No sense in you running around when I have to bring supplies over there already."

"Thank you so much. The bride and groom ordered five cases, but I threw in another case for them to take home as a reminder of their special day."

"Aren't you just the sweetest thing ever Jules."

"You know me, I love watching couples celebrate their love. It wasn't too long ago that I didn't think I'd ever celebrate Jackson and me but thankfully you helped make sure we would have many more years together. How are you doing? Still, seeing Hank? Are we going to meet him soon? It's been what about two months now or so?"

"Wow, you are right. It has been that long. Sometimes it feels like it just started but then other times I can't imagine my life without him."

"Hill?"

"What?"

"You sound like someone who has fallen in love. Am I hearing that right? Are you in love with Hank?"

"Hopelessly. Completely. Madly in love with him. Yes. Am I crazy? Sometimes I feel like the other shoe is going to fall and something bad will happen."

"Aw Hilly, just relax and enjoy this time together. I am so happy that you are this happy. You deserve this and so much more. Don't even bring negative worries into the mix. Has he said anything to you about his feelings?"

"Oh yes, he is very verbal about how he feels and I am pretty sure he loves me too."

"Woman! You need to stop keeping secrets. When you have wonderful things going on in your life you need to share them with your best friends so we can be excited for you. Okay?"

"Okay, one of these days I will bring him to something and you can all be in the know."

"I'd like that very much and I'm sure everyone else will be just as happy for you and Hank."

"Yep, Hank." I smile and try not to laugh. I'm hoping she continues to be this happy when she learns that we've been keeping secrets. "I'll grab your wine this week and have it there for you this weekend. Love ya but I gotta go."

"Love ya too Hilly. Be Happy."

I hung up the phone and call over to the winery. I want to set up a time to pick up the cases that Julia ordered for the wedding this weekend.

"Harmony Winery, how can I help you," Margo answers.

"Margo, this is Hillary Greene from A Matter of Taste. Julia asked me to come and grab those cases from you for her wedding this weekend. When is a good time for me to stop by?"

"Hillary, it's so good to hear from you. I'm here all day usually until about dinner time. We were so slow that we decided to pause during our evening hours until the weather breaks a little. No one wants to come out here with this frozen tundra."

"How slow are you?"

"Dead. Not a single person comes once it's dark."

"Margo, how would you feel about a private wine tasting for two? I'm seeing someone and we are keeping it on the down low still so our nosey friends and family don't interrupt. Would you be open to some wine sampling for me?"

"I will do anything for love. Remember when we opened for Noah and Bree? That was so romantic, and he proposed right here in the vines. I tell everyone that story."

"What day works best for you? Since I'm asking you to be open after normal hours I will work around your schedule."

"We are usually here on Wednesdays working on bottling so if that works I can do a tasting for you and have a fruit and cheese board ready."

"Margo, how about this—I bring you and Dan dinner and whatever my date and I will be eating with our tasting."

"Hillary you don't have to do that."

"I want to and you can't say no. Why don't you pick? I can bring you a special chicken pot pie or a meat-heavy lasagna?"

"Is that the same lasagna that I had at the lady's luncheon at Julia's place?"

"The very same."

"Oh, then please bring the lasagna. I've been dreaming of it since November. Shall we see you at six o'clock?"

"Perfect. I will send Griffin over this week to grab those cases. If anything changes, please let me know. I appreciate this because we haven't been able to go out on dates much to avoid gossip."

"Well, I feel honored to be in on the know Hillary and your secret is safe with us. You have bought my silence with lasagna."

"Thank you again, see you next Wednesday night." Grabbing my phone, I sent Garrett a quick text.

Me: Hello darling
Me: I just made a secret date night for us at the winery next week
HankServiceMan: Nice. How'd you manage that?
Me: Called about a wine order for Jules and asked because Margo said they stopped having evening hours because no one comes out in the cold. So I asked, and she said yes. I agreed to bring her my lasagna.
HankServiceMan: Oh, nice trade. Your lasagna is even better than Jules-but I will deny that forever
Me: Awww-so sweet. Of course, I will have to tell her that.
HankServiceMan: Deny, Deny, Deny
HankServiceMan: Love you, how's your day?
Me: Good, but busy. I have to go but wanted to tell you to reserve Wednesday for a date night!!!
HankServiceMan: On my calendar then let's hit the hot tub before bed because you, after a bunch of wine samples, means extra frisky Hilly for me *winking emoji*
Me: You know you love it and can't wait for it
HankServiceMan: YEP, don't work too hard
Me: Don't arrest anyone

I got up and head out to the front to look for Griffin. He's sitting at the front desk with his earbuds in and singing silently to whatever the hell he is listening to. "Griff." Nothing. I go over and poke him in the shoulder, and he quickly spins and looks at me.

"HEY HILLYBEAN, WHAT'S UP?"

Pointing at his ears, "TAKE THOSE OUT!" I wait until he turns the music off and pulls the earbuds out. "Jesus, how do you have any hearing left? What were you just lip sinking anyway?"

"Annie."

"What? Like the orphan?"

"Yes, Hilly…Little Orphan Annie. The soundtrack."

"I don't even want to, but I have to ask why."

"I'm studying up on my Broadway tunes for the next trivia night at Coopers Corner."

"Of course, you are. Anyway, we have six cases of wine to grab for Jules for the wedding this weekend. Can you do that sometime before the weekend for me? Margo and Dan are usually at the winery until dark."

"Oh yes, I can. I haven't been there lately. Maybe I will do a mini-tasting while I am there and catch up with Margo."

"What is a mini-tasting?"

"It's when I have a glass of their sparkling wine *Drink Happy Thoughts* in a tasting glass, and she refills it for me twice. I love all the names of their wines, but that tastes the best to me. Or their mead, or their table red. Shit, I guess I like all of them." He looks at me and lifts his shoulders.

"Glad you aren't planning on drinking on the job," I said to him sarcastically.

"Aw, do you want to come with me and have a mini-tasting too?"

"Yes, when should we go? What do you have left to do today? Or are you done and just sitting here studying?"

"I was just finishing up Annie and was about to move into Cats, but you spared me more work. It's almost four so I think we worked long enough today."

"Me too. Let me just let G know quick."

"Good idea, tell him not to pull us over for a DUI. It's so awesome that you are doing the nasty with our Sherriff. Let's get you some wine and talk about that a little more."

Chapter Forty-One

Garrett

It's Friday and I just left work to go hang with Cooper while I wait for Hillary to finish her event tonight. She said she was setting it up but that once the food was served, she could leave and her staff would finish up and handle the cleanup. I finished my day, went home to get out of uniform and I'm now sitting at my spot at the bar having wings and beer with my best friend.

"I am not sure if I should feel honored to have you back so soon or be annoyed because it's most likely because your other half has an event," Coop says to me.

"Both. You should always be honored to spend time with me and yes, she is getting the event going but then she will let her staff finish it off. Since I had a free Friday and knew you'd be sitting behind the bar, I thought I would come to eat wings, drink a beer or two and catch up. That all right with you?"

"Sure is. Things good with you?"

"Yeah, work hasn't been too bad outside this cold we have lately. There were some issues with the fire hydrants and gas meters being buried in snow but between Gertie's Facebook post about how to clean those up and the village crew we seem to be in a better position there. My personal life is good. Really good and that's part of why I am here."

"Oh yeah, what's up?"

"I'm going to ask Hillary to marry me."

"I thought we already established that's where this is going?"

"It is but it's happening soon. I am going ring shopping this weekend. Do you think you could go with me?"

Cooper is standing behind the bar with his hands propped on the edge of the bar, "I'm in. When do you want to go?"

"I can go Sunday if that's easier for you. Hillary has that renewal wedding at Harte of Harmony, so I don't have to make excuses about where I am. I think she is there most of the afternoon. That should give us time to head into the city. I don't want anyone seeing me buying a ring."

"I'm happy for you G. I think you guys are great for each other. It's nice to see her looking so happy too."

"Thanks, man, I am happy and I feel like I won the best thing there is to win. I finally have the woman of my dreams and she keeps my life very entertaining." My phone buzzes and I check it to see a text from Hill.

SmittenKitten: Wrapping up here. Should be at love shack in an hour.
Me: See you there. Drive carefully
SmittenKitten: xoxo will do. Love you
Me: Love you too

I look up to see Cooper smiling at me, "You are a man in love. I take it that was Hill?"

"Yeah, give me one more beer and then I'm heading home. She should be there by then."

***

I see that Hillary beat me here. Her car is in the garage, but the hood is still warm. She hasn't been here too long. I'm barely in the kitchen when I feel myself starting to get hit by targets. *What the hell?*

"I'm going to give you twenty seconds to get your own loaded Nerf gun before I continue my attack." She turns around and runs away while I hear her counting down, "Fifteen, fourteen..." shit Where is my gun? There it is on the table. I grab it and strategically go in search of my invader.

I see her shoes behind the curtain and slowly get ready to aim and fire when I feel targets hitting me on the back of the head. "What the hell?"

"AH HA! Never doubt your opponent's ability to be sneaky!"

I move the curtain from the wall and see she has put her shoes there to fake me out. Okay, little lady game on!

***

After a quick round of Nerf gun attacks, we settled down on the couch together. Hillary climbs into my lap, "That was fun. I think I beat you."

"You never cease to amaze and surprise me. What made you think to have a surprise attack against an Army Ranger?"

"Just trying to do something fun that you may like."

"Gotcha, so my beautiful girl, is there more on your agenda tonight or are we going to just relax and watch a movie."

"Ah, tonight begins our weekend of The Movie Challenge."

"Is this more about knowing every little detail of each other in case of a zombie apocalypse?"

"Oh lover, I still have to determine if we are truly compatible. We have not discussed our favorite movies. Tonight, we will begin our movie challenge by watching each other's favorite scary movie, then moving into romance, action, adventure, comedy, and documentary."

"Good lord, you want to watch movies all weekend?"

"Yes, but there is a twist. Whoever wins their choice as the better movie gets to tell the other person what they want. There is also popcorn and movie candy available."

"When I win the better movie I can tell you what I am going to do to you?"

"Yes, or what do you want me to do to you."

"I'm in. what's first…scary movie? My favorite is Misery. When she smashes his feet. Jesus, that's brutal. You?"

"All I have to do is dangle sexy times in front of you and you just agree to anything huh?"

225

"Yep, now what's your movie of choice?"

"The Shining with those creepy ass twins."

"Awesome choice, you win."

Hillary starts laughing, "G, we need to actually watch the movies. Then we vote."

"Let's get this movie challenge started then. Glad you started with four hours of you being scared."

"You want me to be scared?"

"No, I want you snuggled up in my arms where I will keep you safe and love on you."

"You are on. After that, we move into the sappy chick flicks. I'm going to grab our popcorn and candy, be right back."

I take the time to pull up the first movie on a streaming channel, "Found the movie."

Hillary comes back into the family room with snacks, drinks, and our big snuggle blanket, "Okay, I'm ready now. Time to be scared." She snuggles into me and I put my arm around her. "Love you G."

"Love you too baby, you ready to watch this psycho go after the author?"

"Let's do this."

***

We sat through two scary movies with Hillary as close to me as possible. Hey, I'm not complaining. "So, out of the two which do you feel is the scarier one?"

"All I'm going to say is thank fuck I am sleeping here with you tonight because there is no way that I would sleep alone tonight. That was scary as fuck."

"Aw, I promise to keep you safe from ghosts and crazies. But what do you think? I'm still leaning toward Misery being scarier. They both had crazies but in Misery she was nuts. Here he thinks that someone helped him but instead, she is crazy and hurts him to keep him there."

"I'm going to agree with you this time. She was nuts! When she smashes his feet so he can't leave I wanted to throw up."

Rubbing my hands together being pleased with myself that I won the first movie I say, "Winners choice is that you lose your panties during the next one."

Hillary looks me over, "I will do you one better," she stands up, "Since we just sat through almost four hours of movies I think it's time for bed and I plan on sleeping naked." Before she is out of the room, she has her shirt off, bra off, and pants falling off her hips. "Hurry up G, I'm going to be naked before I get to the bed."

Chapter Forty-Two

Hillary

Tonight is our date night at the winery and I am so excited. Garrett and I never get to have date nights, at least not outside the house, yet still in town. Maybe keeping us a secret was a good idea at first but now it's starting to keep us from having a good time because no one knows we are dating. Since it's so cold outside, I can't dress up sexy and be pretty in a dress and heels without freezing my ass off. Winter in Lake Harmony is all about making sure you are warm and safe when you head out of the house. Granted, I'm only going from my place to the winery and back, but I've learned to always be prepared so I am wearing my skinny jeans and a soft warm sweater. I'm meeting Garrett at the love shack now and then we are heading there together. I have the lasagna in a warming bag with bread and a Caesar salad. I left the same here for us since we are just doing a quick tasting and then leaving to come home to enjoy a late dinner.

I watch as he walks into the kitchen after cleaning up, "You ready to head out to the winery baby?"

"Yep, I'm all set. You look sexy in that sweater. I love the way it hugs your shoulders."

He grabs me and pulls me tight, "Thank you and you look beautiful yourself and I love when you wear these jeans. They make your ass look awesome. I want to take a bite of it later."

"Promises, promises, I kiss his lips softly. Let's go enjoy some wine and then I'll bring you home for your own lasagna dinner."

"God woman, you know how to bring me to my knees. Wine tasting, lasagna, and naked time. Perfect."

"Naked time, who said that?"

"It's always implied. Let's go enjoy ourselves on a date!"

He drives us over to the winery and takes the warming bag then turns to help me out of the car next. "What a gentleman, thank you. I can grab the salad and bread in that bag if you carry the lasagna in for me."

We walk into the winery and Dan and Margo, the owners, are behind the counter preparing our tasting. Both look up as we come through the door and their eyes move from me to Garrett. Putting two and two together themselves.

"Now, this is a great surprise," Margo says. "You wouldn't spill the beans when you were here with Griffin last week, but this is a great surprise. How are you, Sherriff?"

"Hey Margo, I'm good but tonight I'm just Garrett. I hear you opened for us to have a date and that was very kind of you. As Hillary must have told you, we were trying to keep things on the down low for a bit. It's nice to be able to take her out and have a real date night."

"Let's get you two over there at that cute romantic table for two and I will bring over your tasting," Dan says.

Hillary kisses my cheek, "Before we go sit down, I want to get your dinner to you. I brought lasagna, Caesar salad, and some fresh rolls. If you want to bring us some tastings and then enjoy your dinner, we can manage for a bit so you can eat while it's hot."

"You are so generous for bringing dinner, Hillary. Margo hasn't stopped talking about this lasagna since her lady's luncheon, so I am expecting a delicious meal. I can't wait!"

"Come on then, let's get this dinner ready. G let me get the food out for them and then I will join you."

"Take your time baby. I will just sit here, enjoy the quiet, and relax."

Margo helps me bring the salad and bread to the back while Dan grabs the lasagna. As we walk into their workroom Margo whispers to me, "I love him for you Hillary. Garrett is such a nice man and boy oh boy the way his eyes follow you. That man is so in love with you!"

"Thanks, Margo, we've known each other since we were kids, but this relationship is new. Sometimes I feel like he's my other half, but I didn't realize it before because he's always been there."

Dan walks over, "Not to eavesdrop on your conversation but Margo and I were neighbors. I can't remember a time that she wasn't there. We dated other people and went to different colleges but neither of us ever met someone else that fit. Maybe the two of you are a little bit like us?"

"You may be right. We aren't going to be here long but the two of you enjoy dinner while it's still warm. If you want to, bring us some tastings or even just a bottle of your cabernet. I brought some cheese and salami for Garrett to nibble on, but we had lasagna waiting for us at home too. We just wanted to take advantage of a date night out. So, thank you both again, very much."

"Absolutely Hillary and don't worry, your secret is safe with us, right Dan," Margo elbows him in the ribs.

Dan puts his arm around Margo, "I know nothing. Let's eat."

I head back into the front of the shop and see Garrett standing and looking out the window into the vines. I walked up to him and put my arms around him and lean against his back.

"Hey baby, are they all set?"

"Yep, they're going to bring some drinks out to us and then eat their dinner before it gets cold."

"They sure have a beautiful place here. When it warms up and we aren't being secretive, we should do a date night here with the gang."

"That would be fun. Let's enjoy some delicious vino and then we can get you back to the house for your dinner."

"And hot tub naked time."

"You are still on your kick of getting me into the hot tub? After eating lasagna?"

"If you are worried about sinking I promise to keep your head above water. I just want you naked and under the stars."

"When you make it sound so romantic how can I refuse."

***

After a lovely evening at the winery and my delicious food for dinner, I caved and agreed to get into the hot tub with a very large glass of water. "I am so thirsty."

"Hill, you drank nearly the entire bottle of red wine. I was going to refill my glass and the bottle was empty."

"It's so good and I was so happy to be out on a date with you and showing you off, and not being worried about it."

"Sounds to me like we have some thinking to do. Do you think it's time to come clean? We've been dating quietly for two months. We love each other and I don't think that will change. What do you want to do?"

I climb into his lap and put my arms around his neck and play with his hair. "What do I want to do? I want to love you forever G. I want to go to sleep with you every night and wake up with you every morning. I want to have Nerf gun attacks, watch movies together, and be with our friends together as a couple. I think that's what I want. What do you want?"

"I want to love you forever."

I kiss him again and then just look into his eyes. I'm going to do it. I'm Hillary fucking Greene and I can do whatever I want. I bite my lip, is this what he will want though, if I am wrong then we end up where we started.

"Hill, when you're quiet like this, it kind of terrifies me. I see the wheels turning but I'm not sure how to read this moment. Talk to me, baby. What's on your mind."

"Garrett, I don't want to hide us anymore. I love you and I believe you love me back?" He nods his head yes and kisses me. "Since we have spent the last two months not only as friends but as lovers- and you have passed all of my get-to-know-you adventures with flying colors- I think there is only one thing left to do."

He is just watching me and not saying a word so here goes, "Garrett, will you marry me?" His smile grows so big it's from one ear to the next but he doesn't say anything. Nothing. "You, you haven't answered me yet."

"Oh Hillary Greene, you can't even allow me to propose to you? You go ahead and ask me first?"

"Yes, but that may be retracted if you don't answer promptly G. I am not kidding around here right now."

"Yes, yes, a million times I will marry you. Although…this is not our formal proposal. I will let you get away with this but a traditional proposal where a man asks a woman is still happening. You just happened to beat me to it. I suppose I shouldn't be surprised."

"Yes? You will marry me. Are you sure?"

"Hillary, I want to marry you more than my next breath. I love you so much and I told you, I am not ever letting you go."

"I love you too G. So, SO much. I think I always have but I don't ever want to be without you again."

"Now, I need to ask you something. Julia is planning a couple's night for Valentine's Day in two weeks. I think we should use that as our coming out party."

"You my sneaky, crazy, husband to be. I love that idea and it is going to blow their minds. Let's do that."

***

The next afternoon we are both at work and I have an idea. I grab my phone to touch base with Garrett. I think we need at least one longer dragged-out and annoying message with all our friends.

Me: Hey lover. I think we need to do one more dragged-out annoying text chain with the gang. You ready!

233

HankServiceMan: you start, I will follow your lead
Me: Thanks, baby. Love you *heart eye emoji*
HankServiceMan: Love you too baby

Me: Hi all, hope you are enjoying your day. Jules-did you already make reservations at Bella Roma's for Valentine's Day???
Julia: I was just going to make them but we decided to do Saturday night instead of actually Vday on Sunday. Since their space is so small we would take up a big portion of their seating.
SmittenKitten: I would like to come and bring a plus 1
Bree: Ohhh are we finally going to meet Hank?
Sam: OMG really???
HankServiceMan: Hey wait a sec. Who's turn, is it? Hill, I was just going to ask Jules if I could have a plus 1 that day
Jackson: Oh man
Rob: This is an interesting dilemma. I think it was Hilly's turn.
Noah: I don't know whose turn it is. This is dumb
Cooper: I thought it was G's turn
Ellen: Scott and I think it's Hilly's turn but may be wrong -Dunno?
SmittenKitten: Well, I suppose I can give the night to Garrett and let Hank and I can do something else for Vday
Julia: Wait, wait. I am not sure whose turn it is but I want to meet Hank
Cooper: G's
Rob: Hilly's
Griffin: why don't you take turns? Hilly gets apps/salads and Garrett can have a meal and dessert.
Rob: Could that work?
Cooper: Why should G have to split his date night? Weird
Rob: Weird for Hill and Hank too
Jackson: Kids...settle down. Can't you both just come? Sit at opposite ends?
SmittenKitten: I don't know. That makes things weird for our significant other, doesn't it?

Me: That would make it horrible sitting at opposite ends of the table
SmittenKitten: See. It's okay guys. Garrett can bring his plus 1 this time and I will come on the next outing.
Julia: If that's what you two agreed on I guess so
Bree: I miss you guys. This is getting old but okay
SmittenKitten: Enjoy your dinners and I hope you are nice to Garrett's date.
Julia: Of course!

***

SmittenKitten: You just earned yourself a BJ
Me: Love you baby...I am laughing so hard! Idiots.
SmittenKitten: Yes, but they are our idiots.
Me: Rob, Cooper, and Griff...omg. Dying
SmittenKitten: They are rockstars. Stir that pot boys!

Chapter Forty-Three

Garrett

The week is flying by fast, but I have one more surprise up my sleeve for Hillary. I know she doesn't have anything going on Thursday through Saturday of this week, so I've planned something special for her with Griffin's help. This delivery is going to be taken to her by me personally. I stand up from my desk, grab my coat and the small envelope and hide it under my coat. By the way my nosey crew is I don't need them getting suspicious. Griffin has Hillary over at the winery again for mini tastings. I worked with Dan and Margo, and we lined one of the rows of vines with twinkling lights.

I hurried home to change my clothes into something warm and head over to the winery. I know there aren't a lot of customers because they aren't very busy. Griff sees my car pull up through the window. He has strategically put Hillary with her back to the window. I know that Noah proposed here to Bree, but when you aren't allowed to show your face in public together options are limited. I take a deep breath and get out of my car and head to the tasting room.

As I walk in, I watch Griff smirk and excuse himself. He is going to record this on his phone since I want a memory of it. I slowly bend down and kiss her head, "Hi sweetheart. Mind if I sit down?"

"Hi, what a nice surprise. How'd you get off work early? Are you going to take your big coat off and stay?"

"Actually, can you put your coat on and get warm, I want to show you something."

"Um, okay."

She stands up and I help her into her coat. She wraps her scarf around her and puts on her cute hat and mittens. "Where are we going?"

"Come on, it's a secret." I grab her hand and smile as I pass Margo. She gives me a wink. We start walking towards the vines.

"G I am not sure that we are supposed to go wandering through the vines. These vines are like their babies."

"Hill, it's okay come on." We get about twenty feet into the vines and the lights flicker on.

"Oh, how pretty. What's going on? What are you up to mister."

I pulled the envelope out of my pocket and handed it over to her. "I have a surprise for you. I'm not sure if you will agree with me, and if not, we can make different arrangements."

"Just hand it over." She grabs the envelope quickly from my hands. I watched her open it and pull out two airplane tickets.

"G…before I jump to conclusions, I think you better give me an idea of what this is. Two airplane tickets to Vegas?"

I pull the ring box from my other pocket, and get down on one knee, "They go along with this surprise." I open the ring box and a shining ring sits there. "Hillary Greene, marry me. Let's run away to Vegas and get married tomorrow. I don't want to wait another day to call you my wife."

Her eyes are glossy and I watch as a tear falls down her cheek. "YES! Yes, I will marry you and yes let's go to Vegas baby. I can't wait to be your wife."

She pulls me up and I put the ring on her finger and kiss her. "I love you, Hillary. Are you sure about Vegas? I don't want to take the dream of a big white wedding away from you."

"Babe, I am one hundred percent sure. I don't want to wait. I don't want to plan a big event. I do that every day. Let's just make it the two of us and then when we get back, we will let my parents throw us a big party. Let them plan it and handle all the details and we can just go and enjoy the party."

"If you are sure, then let's go. I love you, baby."

"I love you too and I LOVE this ring."

"I made sure to tell the jeweler that you were a chef so that she could help me pick the perfect ring. She thought something without a lot of open spaces would be the best choice. When I saw this one with the three princess-cut diamonds it called to me. It's like one for you, one for me, and one for us."

"You are a beautiful romantic man. The ring is beautiful. Now we have only one problem left. Can we have Elvis marry us?"

"Absolutely. I wouldn't have expected you'd want anything else."

***

We flew into Vegas this morning after our engagement last night at the winery. Little did we know but Margo and Dan had sparkling wine, strawberries, and chocolate fondue waiting for us when we came back inside. Griffin waited long enough to take some more pictures, give us both hugs and kisses and promised to keep our secret. He is also covering for Hillary while we are out and I'm hoping no one realizes I took the days off.

The flight got us in at eleven in the morning. Hillary and I are staying at the Wynn and it's stunning. I called Jax Turner, our very own Mr. Hollywood, to see if he could get us into the Delilah restaurant here in the Wynn which is incredibly difficult to get a reservation for, and not only does he have a table for two reserved for us but he upgraded our room to a tower suite which has eighteen hundred square feet of high end living. It has a spacious living room with a dining area and wet bar, a huge king bed, and a fancy marble bathroom. Hillary already decided we will be enjoying the deep soaker tub with champagne before we leave tomorrow.

Hillary ran off to the bathroom to get ready after I came out of the bathroom. We are getting married by Elvis at four o'clock this afternoon. We decided to splurge on the wedding and got the official Ultimate Elvis Wedding experience which includes a limo to and from the Chapel, Elvis officiating, 3 songs of his greatest hits, a white rose bouquet and boutonniere, and photos and video of the wedding.

I must admit I'm a little bit nervous but only because I want to make the day perfect for her. I was relieved to not have to wait and go through the ordeal of planning a wedding. I feel like I've waited my whole life for this day, and I don't want to wait another minute to call her my wife, Mrs. Hillary Stone. She doesn't know it, but I did go speak to her parents. They knew we had been dating because Hillary doesn't keep secrets from them. Her dad gave me the traditional okay to ask her to marry me. They were both extremely happy to hear that we were getting married. They said they always considered me one of their own, so I got a little bit emotional during that discussion. They are excited to be able to plan the reception without any worries. The only thing we need to do is tell them whom to invite. We both agreed we'd keep it semi-small but that will most likely include most of the town because of our jobs and how involved we both are with the community.

Now I am sitting here feeling a little guilty about not telling my parents. I go over and knock on the door of the bathroom. "Hill… I am not coming in but I'm going to call my mom and dad quickly and let them know what's going on, okay."

She cracks the door and pokes her head out, "You didn't tell them? Do you want to wait and do a real wedding with them?"

"No, I honestly only told Coop. Rob figured it out when we were away over New Year's but I haven't told Mom and Dad and now I'm feeling guilty about it but NOTHING is going to stop this wedding today."

"Aw, babe don't feel bad. Do you want to call them together? I can come out and talk to them with you."

"I love you, baby. I appreciate that but it's our wedding day and I don't want to interrupt you. I'll go sit in the other room and give them a call while you keep getting ready."

"Okay, but are you sure?"

"Yeah, thank you but I can fill them in. I love you."

"Love you too. Come here and kiss me."

I walk over to the door, and she sticks her face out of the bathroom more. I kiss her softly on the lips. "Thank you for loving me and making me the happiest man in the world."

"You are so easy to love G. Now go make yourself feel better and give your folks a call. Tell them I love them, and we will come to see them when we get home."

God this woman. I love her and she understands me. I grabbed my phone and gave my mom a call.

"Hello Garrett, how are you today?"

"Hey Mom, I'm good. Are you home with Dad right now?"

"Yes, is everything okay honey?"

"Yes, everything is great, but can you go get him and put me on speaker? OH wait, are you guys home alone?"

"I'm with your dad and we are home alone. Go ahead and tell me what has you upset."

"This may come as a surprise, but I am in Vegas with Hillary right now and we are getting married today." I sit and wait and don't hear anything coming from the other end of the call. "Hello, are you guys there?"

"Hello son, we're here but your mom is all choked up. So, it's your big wedding day and you and Hilly are getting married."

"Yes, are you upset Mom?"

"No baby, I am not upset, in fact, I am extremely happy for you. For you both. These are big happy tears. You know that we love Hilly like our own. I always thought you had feelings for her but I didn't realize that she felt the same way. Can you fill your dad and me in a little bit because we are still processing the news? Last we knew you guys weren't doing things together and I know Julia was getting pretty upset thinking she ruined your friendship with each other after the cabin fiasco."

"Ah, the cabin. That's about where this all started. We actually cleared the air and I told her I was in love with her. We decided to try dating and being in a relationship but without the opinions or interference from everyone else.

We've been dating in secret since then and we just decided not to waste any more time and I proposed and now here we are being married by Elvis in about two hours."

I hear my mom's sniffles and my dad clears his throat, "Son, we are both so excited and happy for you. Elvis huh? You went to Vegas and are getting married by Elvis. Does everyone else know now?"

"No, we need you to keep it a secret for another week. We are telling the gang next weekend at the Valentine's Day dinner. We are going to show up together as husband and wife."

Laughing in the background, "Oh boy, Garrett your sister is going to kill you! Edison, can you believe these kids of ours? I don't want to be anywhere near you when you tell your sister. She will be happy for the both of you of course but be ready for her and all of them to be a little bit upset about all the secrets."

"Yeah, we know and we are prepared but I'm going to be honest and tell you that it was worth it."

My parents are both laughing, "Oh son, you are going to have one heck of a life being married to Hilly. I love you both but just remember-a happy wife happy life. Now, go enjoy your wedding day, and do not feel bad about it."

"Thank you, I was feeling a bit guilty for not having told you and even though we are doing the wedding here we will be having a reception at home. Hill's parents are going to plan it and handle it because she doesn't want to make a big fuss. I think they would love knowing that you both know."

"That is perfect. As soon as we hang up with you we are going to invite her parents over to have some champagne and talk about how your dad and I can pitch in on the reception."

Feeling a lot better and relieved to have this secret off my chest with my parents I finish the call, "Hill is getting ready and we promise to come to see you when we get home. Just remember, mums the word for another week. After Valentines Day you can share the news with whomever you want."

"We love you and Hilly very much and wish you a wonderful wedding day. Kiss her from us please."

"I will. Thank you both for understanding, now I better go get myself dressed and ready to go before my bride beats me to it."

Chapter Forty-Four

Hillary

I keep humming to myself *Going to the chapel and we're… gonna get married… by Elvis*. So maybe those aren't the exact words, but it is all true so there. *Holy shit, I am getting married today*. Poor Garrett. He looked so torn that he hadn't told his parents. I probably should have made sure that both of our parents were aware of what we were doing. Well, he is telling them now and it will make him happy and hopefully, they will be happy for us too. His parents have always been a second set of parents to me.

I glance at my dress in the mirror which is hanging behind me on the glass shower door. I bought this dress intending to wear it for Valentine's Day but now that we are here having this crazy wedding with Elvis, I want to wear it today. It's a gorgeous red silk cocktail dress that is tasteful but still sinful. Who said a bride must wear white? I mean...come on, because I sure as hell am not a virgin. This silky dress is a sheath style with a floral embroidered illusion neck with beading and lace. It has silk and lace and all that is required for a wedding dress. I'll wear my four-inch silver stiletto heels with it and bam, here comes the bride.

I carefully apply my makeup and keep it classy and simple. I don't want to wear too much in case I cry and make a mess of myself. Garrett loves to kiss me so I don't want to have bold lips either. I love when he kisses me like he is going to ravish me and can't get enough. All done and it's almost time for the limo to pick us up. I look in the mirror from side to side and do a little shimmy.

Opening the door he is standing at the open window admiring the view from our windows. He's wearing a dark blue suit that looks impressive on him. He turns and the blue in his suit brings out the deep blue of his eyes. My fiancé, soon-to-be husband stands staring at me with his hands in his pockets. He is so delicious I can't wait to get my hands on him later.

"Wow, aren't you handsome G. I can't wait to marry you and call you my husband. How many tears this shall cause all those single ladies at home."

"Come here," he says and is pulling me near with his finger. "Now do a little spin for me, baby. I want to see how good your ass looks in this dress."

I do a little spin, very slowly, and when my back is to him I look over my shoulder with a smirk and do a little shimmy. "You like?"

"I do. You are the most beautiful bride I have ever seen. May I kiss you or will I mess up your lips?"

"Oh, please. Please kiss me before I explode."

He pulls me into his chest and runs his thumb along my jawline, "You have made me the happiest man in the world and I promise to make you the happiest woman in the world."

"Wow, the happiest couple in the world. That is an impressive declaration. Will we be happier than Jules and Jackson?"

"Yes."

"Happier than Bree and Noah?"

"Yes."

"Sam and Paul?"

"Yes."

"Ellen and Scott?"

"Yes."

"The biggest one…happier than your parents?"

"Yes, and all of those are very big shoes to fill but we will be happier than all of them put together because I love you with all my heart and that will never change. Whatever you want in the world, I will give you. Whatever you need, I will find. It's just that simple."

"I love a big, sexy, strong man, with confidence. Okay, I will marry you. I promise to be the wife you so deserve. I promise to not always make you crazy. To be patient and understanding. To give you whatever it is that you want and need." I kiss him.

"I think that we should go downstairs now, find our limo, and have Elvis sing us a love song or two and marry us because I can't wait another minute for you to be Mrs. Stone."

"Oh, that is lovely, but what about Mr. Greene."

"No."

"No? Is this our first fight as a married couple?" I laugh as he pulls me out of the room and towards our future.

***

Sitting in the limo heading to the chapel for the wedding and I'm snuggled up against Garrett's chest. I can feel his heart pounding, "Are you doing okay there handsome?"

"Yes, why do you ask that?"

"I can feel your heart beating and I am checking to see if you are going to have a heart attack or something."

"Would you believe me if I told you it was excitement and not nerves?"

I swivel a little bit to look at his face. "Yes, I do believe it is excitement but you have an alarming smile across your face. You aren't going to stroke out on me, are you? Do you have a life insurance policy? Oh my god G, we didn't go over that stuff. Do not die on me now okay."

He starts laughing, "Hill, please promise me that whatever you do, you do not change. I want you to continue to be this crazy, think before she speaks, woman because I love that part of you."

"Fine, but when we get home Mr. Greene we will be talking about our wills, and life insurance policies, and I suppose we have to figure out where we will be living."

"We can live wherever you want to live and yes, we can figure out all that other stuff. I promise."

"I want to live closer to the girls. Can we sell both of our places and buy something bigger, closer to Jules and Bree?"

"Whatever you want to do baby. I'm good with whatever you decide as long as we have a nice place big enough to have all our friends over."

"Oh look, I think we are here. That looks like a creepy Elvis waving at us from the chapel."

"That is one hell of a creepy ass Elvis. We got the fat Elvis at the end of his career."

We hear the limo driver chuckle up front as we come to a stop and Elvis opens the door serenading us with Love Me Tender. "You ready?" I asked Garrett.

"Let's make you, my wife."

Chapter Forty-Five

Garrett

It's been a week of wedded bliss, lots of sex, and more decisions. After we came back from our wedding in Vegas, we met up with both of our parents at Hillary's parents' home. My parents are all into this secret romance now and think it's the best news in the world that Hillary is officially part of the family. Decisions have started about the reception, and they wanted to know when we want to celebrate and whom we want to invite. We told them sometime in the next couple of months is fine, and that we'd get a list of names to them by the end of the week. From there, they have the power to do the rest except we ruled against a Vegas-Elvis-themed party when they sprang that on us.

Hillary and I decided to work with my dad on a new build that is close to Bree and Noah's house. It is almost ready for occupancy and we both like the craftsman style, plus Dad is still able to put a deck and screened porch on the back for us. Once we have that ready, we can sell both our places. For now, Hillary decided I should move in with her because I have less stuff to physically move. Once I'm out we list my place and then once we move into our new place, we list hers.

She also made sure that all legal paperwork, including our wills and any life insurance policies, have each other's names on them. She doesn't realize it, but I also put the military money I have in my portfolio in her name too. I don't ever want her to worry about anything again.

Tonight is the Valentine's Day dinner at the Italian restaurant with all our friends. Jules thinks I am bringing whomever I have been dating, but instead, Hillary and I are going to show up late and together and act like nothing is different. Once they realize that we are Hank and Smitten

Kitten we are going to wait to see how long it takes for them to notice our rings.

"I think we should make a bet on how they react," Hill says.

"What? Their reaction to us coming in together?"

"Yeah, I think we stroll in together, not all lovey-dovey but normal, sit down together and not say anything. Their reaction to that."

"I imagine they will have some questions. But I'd like to change the bet. Let's bet on how many minutes it takes for them to see we got married."

She looks over with her typical snarky smirk, "You are on big guy. I bet it will take them at least eight minutes to see the rings and ask."

"I am going to bet less than eight, but you can't hide your hand. You have to leave it on the table and act like normal."

"I will never hide this beautiful ring and what it means to me ever again. We are officially coming out of the closet tonight! But…more important is WHAT are we betting," she asks me.

"Lover's choice?"

"No, we did that last time. Let's make it a foot and back massage."

"You think you are going to win and get those massages huh."

"Yep."

"Make sure we take all those Elvis wedding photos we have in our gold sparkly wedding album. It should fit in your purse. That way when they get upset that they weren't included you can pass it to Jules and the girls to look at as a consolation bribe."

"Damn, I married a smart man. Are you ready to go? They should all be there by now. I'm excited but scared. How pissed do you think they will be?"

"They'll get over it, let's go beautiful. I want to show off my wife."

"Let's go Mr. Greene."

"Baby, you do realize that I am not Mr. Greene and will never be, but you are one sexy and beautiful Mrs. Stone."

"That I am but I like calling you Mr. Greene."

"You like to harass me with it."

She stands up on her toes and kisses me, "That too."

***

We arrive at Bella Roma a quaint little Italian restaurant owned by Maria and Antoni. The restaurant only seats about 40 people and so with our big group, we take up most of the room. The two of us pause outside the main door and look in to see all our friends seated around a large table. Julia and Jackson, Bree and Noah, Sam and Paul, Ellen, and Scott, and even Rob and Cooper are here.

"You ready?"

"Yes, let's go blow their minds, mister."

Hillary walks in with a flourish and heads to one of the empty seats. I walked in behind her and take the empty seat next to her. We both say hello but there is no talking coming from our table. I look up and see Julia trying to put the situation into something understandable. "Happy Valentine's Day everyone. I hope you weren't waiting for me." Still no words. I look around at all our friends as I sit down. Rob and Coop are sitting there not saying a word. Good job guys. I haven't given you the all-clear yet.

Julia sits up tall and looks over at Jackson. He gives a shoulder shrug. Then she looks at Bree who also seems a bit confused. Then finally my sister looks over at me and asks, "It's nice to see the both of you at the same place without an issue. I thought you were going to bring a date, Garrett?"

"I did bring a date. I brought Hill."

Hill smiles at her, "Isn't that nice? Do you want me to leave?"

Julia still looking a bit confused, "No Hill, of course, I don't want you to leave. I guess I am confused because I thought that Garrett was bringing whomever he has been dating and I thought you were going out with Hank."

Almost at the same time, I say, "I did."

While Hill says, "I am."

Dead silence for about a minute until Rob and Cooper can't hold it together any longer. Rob finally takes the moment to stand up and tell our table, "Everyone, I'd like to introduce you to Hank and his Smitten Kitten."

Hillary and I sit there and smile and then she grabs the back of my head and gives me one hell of a kiss in front of all our friends. We start to hear clapping and when we pull apart, we notice that not only are our friends laughing and clapping but the whole damn restaurant is too. Hillary blushes, and as I look around the room, I notice Gertie and her widow's dinner club ladies in the room too. She gives me a wink and mouths *Can I post about it now?* I nod my head to her and I swear she goes to grab her phone.

The restaurant quiets down and Julia finally has her chance. "Oh my God, you guys. How long has this been going on? Have you been Hank and your Smitten Kitten this entire time?"

Hillary elbows me and says, "Go ahead explain. I'm going to enjoy this glass of wine." With a wink I watch her pick up her glass with her left hand.

"Jules, it started at the cabin. We talked, figured things out."

"He told me he loved me, has loved me," Hillary interrupts.

"Yes, I told Hill I am in love with her and wanted a chance to see where things would go. We decided it would be a lot easier to take that step without the love and interference from all of you-sorry- but it was worth it and now here we are."

"Here you are," Julia adds. "I'd like to make a toast to the both of you then. Everyone lift your glass- to Hillary and Garrett and all the happiness that you both deserve. May you learn to not keep big secrets from your best friends or create fake truces ever again. Cheers!"

Everyone toasts and then sees Bree stand abruptly and screams, "JIMENY CRICKETS!"

Of course, everyone is worried it is the baby, Noah is freaking out and Bree is waving her hands trying to catch her breath. "Bree are you okay, what's wrong honey? Is it the baby? Should we go to the hospital," Noah is asking.

Bree stands up and points to Hillary and me back and forth not getting a word out. Finally, she screams, "Are you MARRIED?"

Hillary looks at me with a smirk, "I win. Massages on you tonight." Then she looks across the table at Bree. "Please sit Bree before that baby pops out of you and your husband has a heart attack." She looks around the room, "Okay since you are all listening too, I will say this loud enough for everyone to hear. Garrett and I went to Vegas and got married!"

Maria and Antoni are bringing champagne to our table and the entire restaurant is up and congratulating us. This continues for about fifteen minutes until everyone is back at their table and we can continue our evening as a group again.

Hillary comes over and sits down on my lap putting one arm around me and starts playing with my hair while she speaks to our table. "Before you get upset or have a million questions, I want to tell you all that we love you. Everyone at this table means something special to both of us. We decided we'd wasted enough time and wanted to begin our lives as husband and wife. We went to Vegas and had fat Elvis marry us and now we are home to share our happiness with you. Our moms and dads are planning on throwing us a big reception and we would love for you to be part of that special day. I have our obnoxious but wonderful Elvis Chapel wedding pictures here tonight and the next time we all get together I will show you our wedding video. It will be a wonderful Elvis sing-along night because let me tell you. We got the Elvis performance of a lifetime. Fat Elvis not only sang the three songs we paid for but gave us a few encores.

So…are we good? We are sorry if we kept secrets, but I hope you can agree that the outcome was worth it?”

“Well said, baby. Kiss me.”

Hill leans into me and grabs my face, “I love you, husband.”

“I love you, wife.”

We hear a bunch of awes coming from our friends and while Hill is still kissing me I hear Julia say, “This is going to be weird getting used to but I am happy that my best friend and my brother can be in the same room together again and those damn texts messages are over.”

“Oh my God, you two! Did you do all those stupid text messages of my turn, no it’s my turn, then you go, no you go…that was all bullshit? I kind of hate you both right now.”

Hillary sits back up, “Now Jules, remember what I just said…We are sorry we kept secrets from all of you but isn’t the outcome so worth it? I think so. We are married, in love, and enjoying so many sexy times!”

I hear Cooper, “Oh please don’t get her started on the sexy times. I had to boil my head the last time.”

“Be happy, love each other, and remember the road you took to find each other. I love you both and I forgive you for being a pair of idiots,” Julia adds.

Epilogue

Hillary and I are relaxing on the couch watching another version of Who's Movie is Better and this time it's comedy. Both movies have been pretty good so it's just a matter of choosing a new movie or a classic. The winner gets to use the edible chocolate paint on the other, so I am good with winning or losing.

My phone rings and I see it's Jax Turner calling. "Hey Jax, how are you doing?"

"Garrett, I need your help. This is actually a business call."

"Shit Jax, are you okay? What do you need."

"My best friend is in trouble…it's Sophie. Sophie Knight. I have her at my place right now because she had a break-in at her house yesterday. She didn't alert me to having a stalker and somehow, he managed to get through the gatehouse to her community and her personal gate at the house. By the time the local police arrived, he was gone with some of her personal things and left a shattered front door. She was smart enough to hide and called the police with her cell phone and they kept her on the line until they arrived."

"Jesus! He didn't get to her though, right?"

"No, just took some of her clothes and her pillow from the bed. We aren't sure yet who he is but she's with me right now. She refuses to get personal security like her manager and I have asked her to do so instead I'm hoping I can send her your way and she can hide out in Lake Harmony for a while. She is taking a break between films anyway. We don't want her going to her hometown in Wisconsin because this stalker could head there if he realizes she isn't here in LA anymore. "

"Of course, Jax, you know our community is good to you, and I'm sure they would be good to her. What exactly do you need from me? Do you want me to find someone to be personal security here?"

"No, she won't go for that. My aunt Gertie said that you and Rob have some rental properties. I am hoping we can hide her in one of those and I'll pay to put a security system in place. Once we get her there, she will be off the grid, and with you watching I will feel much better about this whole situation. She is going to use one of my credit cards and has a new cell. Nothing will be traceable. Only you and whomever you trust will know she's even there."

"I've got you, man. So, when is this happening? How are we getting her here?"

"I've got a charter plane bringing her into the county airport there. She is flying in costume so that even the airport employees won't recognize her. I'm really worried about her safety man. I knew I could count on you."

"Jax, of course. This is what we do for friends. As soon as I get off the phone with you, I will give Rob a call. We haven't booked the newest house yet because I was using it, but I think that will be the safest place we have. I will get Rob to get high-end security installed. She will be able to go outside there too because there aren't close neighbors, so she won't feel so isolated. I know once she is here the gang will make sure she doesn't feel alone. Don't worry man, we've got you covered."

"I really appreciate this. She is my best friend. I don't know what I would do if something happened to her."

"Do me one more favor though, before this all goes down. Call your aunt. Gertie cannot post anything about Sophie being here. Any alert at all will trigger social post alerts and if he's a smart stalker he has alerts set for any time something about her posts online."

"Yeah, she's my next call. I know I can trust her to not say anything but even posting to not harass Sophie while she's there would defeat the purpose of sending her there."

"Glad we are on the same page. I'm going to need to alert my guys so when they are patrolling, they can keep an eye out, but they know protocols and I'm not worried about that."

"I appreciate this so much. I want to keep her here with me for a couple of days to make sure she is okay and not just telling me what I want to hear. That will give you time to get things done. Tell Rob to touch base with me about any costs. I'll cover all of that."

"Got it. Don't worry, between all of us she won't be alone, and we will make sure she is safe."

"Thanks again man, and congratulations. I'm happy for you and Hillary."

"Thank you, I'll let her know."

"Ok, I will make sure to send you flight and arrival information when I have it. Talk to you later."

"Don't worry Jax. We will take good care of her."

Hillary looks over at me, "I think I got the jest of that but want to elaborate. What happened?"

"That was Jax. Sophie Knight has a stalker, and she is coming to hide in the love shack until they figure out who this jackass is and catch him. He broke into her house and stole her clothes and pillow off the bed."

"That's fucking creepy. Gross, he's probably making love to her pillow and smelling her clothes."

"Yeah, Jax was pretty worked up over it because she doesn't seem to be taking this too seriously. He wants her here and totally off the grid. I'll talk to Rob and get him over to the house. We need to add some top-notch security to the house. I figured between all of us we can keep her company and not feel too alone. We just need to keep her away from the public. It's one thing for them to ignore Jax and let him keep some semblance of normal while he is home, but she isn't one of ours. She's still Hollywood's current sweetheart so they won't be as respectful. The bottom line is we must keep her being here in Lake Harmony off social media."

"Is she bringing any security with her?"

"Nope, completely refuses. Doesn't think it's necessary."

"If I need to share you while she's here I am okay with that. Let's just make sure she feels safe and doesn't go stir-crazy being alone too much. This calls for a meeting of the minds with the Board of Knowledge."

"Hilly, you're probably right. Let's see if we can get the gang over to your shop. Let's figure out a plan and a schedule. I know Bree will want to be involved. She already has a friendship with Sophie. I think that was the only thing in Jax's favor of getting her to agree to all this."

"It will be okay. We've got this and you know the girls won't let her be alone. We can strategically make plans to get together. We just need to keep it off the social radar. Is that what all that talk was about Gertie?"

"Yeah, you know Gertie means well, but I didn't even want her posting something about if people saw Sophie to give her space. Sophie's name cannot pop up on social media connecting her to Lake Harmony at all."

"Agreed. I'll see if the gang can meet tonight."

Hillary grabs her phone and starts typing away.

Hillary: Hey all-emergency group meeting. Can you meet us at my shop at 6 pm?
Julia: Is everything okay?
Hillary: All good. A situation that needs discussion and discretion. Time for the White Board of Knowledge
Bree: Ooh...this sounds interesting. Noah and I will be there
Sam: I can make it but Paul can't. see you later
Coop: I can give you 30 min or so
Griffin: Do you need me?
Hillary: 10-4 Griff
Rob: Please promise this isn't one of your crazy pacts
Me: Rob, calling you shortly – answer
Rob: Ohh...interesting indeed
Jackson: Jules and I will be there
Hillary: No kiddo's for this one pls.
Jackson: *thumbs up emoji*
Stella: I'll be there
Ellen: Scott and I can make it

Hillary: Thanks gang...see you there. I can provide a meal- bring your drinks. Again, the situation needs HIGH DESCRETION!!!
Rob: Now you have me really intrigued and excited
Me: Shut up Rob. Answer your damn phone

THE END

Dear Reader,

Thank you for reading Hillary and Garrett's story-**Covert Entanglements**. Want more of this hilarious group of friends? The series continues with Sophie and Jax's story **Healing Forces**, the fourth book in The Lake Harmony Series.

Not ready to leave Hillary and Garrett yet? Click here to get an exclusive BONUS scene or use the QR code!

If you want to start at the beginning and fall in love with Lake Harmony and all its characters read Julia and Jackson's story-**Five Dates**.

Binge the rest of the series Free in Kindle Unlimited!

The Lake Harmony Series:
Five Dates (Julia & Jackson)
Sexy Secrets (Bree & Noah)
Covert Entanglements (Hillary & Garrett)
Star Obsessions (Rob & Sophie) *coming soon!*

About the Author

Tanja Waltrip was born and raised in the 'burbs of Chicago and now resides in sunny Florida. Despite the tumultuous nature of chasing the sun, one thing has remained the same—her voracious reading habit. She always knew that she would one day turn this passion for the Contemporary Romance genre into her own writing pursuit.

Please sign up HERE for my NEWSLETTER to receive news about upcoming releases and giveaways.

I love to interact with my readers, whether it's a plotline critique or a desire to see one of my characters live in infamy, so please don't hesitate to send me a message. Tanjawaltrip.com

Book Links and other content: